Boys Don't Cry

Boys
Don't
Cry

Fíona Scarlett

faber

First published in 2021
by Faber & Faber Limited
Bloomsbury House
74–77 Great Russell Street
London WC1B 3DA

Typeset by Faber & Faber Limited
Printed and bound by CPI Group (UK) Ltd, Croydon, CRO 4YY

A CIP record for this book
is available from the British Library

ISBN 978–0–571–36607–1

10 9 8 7 6 5 4 3 2 1

*For my Da – who continues
to inspire me every day*

Ice cream. Any flavour. Chocolate, banana, strawberry, or that one that has all three striped together, sandwiched in a wafer. A screwball from Mr Whippy with double sauce and sprinkles, begging Ma for a euro and legging it down the concrete steps, praying that I'd get there before he left, following the music-box sounds of 'Greensleeves', or 'Teddy Bears' Picnic', or 'Yankee Doodle Dandy'.

Being pushed in a Tesco trolley round the back of the flats. Joe giving us all a shot, but letting me stay the longest. Pushing me faster. Spinning and laughing while crashing into the overflowing double-steel bins.

Mrs O'Sullivan reading Roald Dahl. *The Witches*. *The Twits*. *Matilda*. Out loud. Putting on the voices. Letting me borrow them after and never asking for them back.

My red Transformer, the one Da got me for my birthday. Even with its left wheel missing and scraped-off face, it was still my favourite.

Swimming in the sea at Dollymount Strand. Making sandcastles then kicking them down. Poking the washed-up jellyfish with a stick and standing on the dead ones.

Ma warming my pyjamas on the bedroom rad, tucking me in, making sure to plug in my Stormtrooper night light. Always.

Joe flying down Captains Hill, with me on the handlebars. Joe sneaking me into 15s films at The Plex, with plastic bags of popcorn, fizzy worms and Coke. Joe sharing his head-phones and turning up the volume when Da took chunks out of Ma.

I still wish they'd let Da visit.

I wish they'd let me home.

I wish they'd serve Big Macs here instead of cabbage, mash and ham.

Dr Kennedy said to write it all down, the things I'll miss the most. It's supposed to be part of the *process*, help me *transition*. But trying to fit everything in that's busting out the top of my head is sending me mental. Plus nobody has come out and said it yet. Not the nurses, not Dr Kennedy, not Ma.

But Joe asked me if I was afraid.

That's when I knew.

Joe

I'm getting closer now and the four towers are in view: Gandhi, Mandela, King and Bojaxhiu. Each tower named after someone who inspired change, hoping that the names would rub off on the dossing sponging bastards who existed there.

Of course we live in Bojaxhiu, or The Jax as it's more fondly known. Could they not just have fucking called it Teresa?

It's a scorcher, which means everyone is out getting that healthy Irish burn. Lads bare-chested, toddlers stripped to their nappies, and little shits out in force with their water guns and balloons soaking anything that moves.

I get to The Jax and enter the stairwell and the heat has just intensified the unidentifiable bang of the place. The rusted Dublin City Council *No Ball Games* sign has finally fallen and is fighting for space amongst the discarded syringes and smokes boxes and dried-in gank.

I used to hide funny messages for Finn amongst the endless scribbles of graffiti plastering the walls. He'd spend hours looking for them, searching between *Tina is a leg opener* and *Anto woz here* and *Jimmy is gay*, and would always answer back. That's how I knew he'd found it, his spider scrawl there right next to mine.

As I'm climbing the stairs David Carthy is in his regular spot, the corner between floors three and four, giving him enough of a head start in either direction if needed. He's all encased in thick sweet smoke and off his head on whatever-the-fuck sample he's helped himself to today. He'd better watch it, Dessie Murphy doesn't do freebies.

'All right, Joe,' David calls out as I pass.

'David,' I say, nodding, and continue on up.

'How's your Da?' he asks.

'Fucked if I know,' I say over my shoulder.

'Well, you can tell him thanks from me. Business is booming since his holiday chez Joy.'

'Looks it, yeah,' I say, and I can see the crimson come to his face and his fist clench but he won't fucking touch me, no one will. They're all afraid of Da.

I push my way through onto the landing of floor ten and the wall of the veranda has been repainted. Wimbledon White, according to the tin. Michael from 101B does the honours twice a year. 'It has to look the part,' he says.

Dessie Murphy may own the stairwells, but we take ownership of our landings. Welcome mats are placed at doors, window boxes hang from ledges, and Josie from 104B has two little porcelain frogs on either side of her entrance, all the way from Santa Ponsa, she says. Our window boxes lie empty. Ma didn't plant them this year.

I take a look over the veranda, squinting at the unusually clear blue skies. Dublin Mountains to the left and Dublin Bay to the right. Fuck, you couldn't pay for that view. In the time before, I'd be legging it in to get Finn and Dart it out to Dollymount; spend the day building sandcastles and swimming in the sea.

I put my key in the door and the smell hits me first, Bacardi and Marlboro Whites, followed closely by the moist, enclosed darkness. I heave apart the curtains, push open the windows and start cleaning up around Ma, who is spread unconscious on the couch. I put one hand behind her head, another across her chest, and roll her onto her side. I get the fleece blanket from Finn's bed, his favourite Captain America one, and place it over her, tucking it in under her chin. I go to the press under the sink, root around for the black sacks, and there it is, right at the back where I'd left it, cobwebbed-forgotten. I reach out to touch it, but pull myself back, not ready yet to face it.

Finn

'Finn, you're in goal.'

'My arse, I was in last time.'

Myself, Jasmine, Dunner and Shane were the first ones there. We flung our school bags under the bench and stripped off our jumpers, running to mark the goalposts.

We always legged it right on the school bell, to get first shot at The Yard. Each block looked onto it, which meant you could get away with nothing, too many Mas' eyes staring out through net curtains. That suited us just fine, it kept the older ones away. As for the younger ones? Well, they could go and shite, we could handle them.

It was supposed to be a garden – well, according to Da anyway – and there was a remnant of a burned-out bench to prove his point. But I was glad the council got bored and decided to leave it as it is. You wouldn't get much football done in a garden, and the wheels of your scooter wouldn't roll, and you'd probably get auld ones just sitting in it, looking at stuff. No, I much preferred it as it was, all concrete and gated; it kept it just for us.

'Penos?' Dunner asked while taking twelve steps away from goal, trying to mark a spot in the cracking pavement with his heel. 'Not beyond here or I'll call cheat!' he warned, and a Dunner warning was enough. Not that he'd do anything, mind you, but he was just such a moan hole that he'd go on and on about it for ages and drive us all demented.

'Right so, who's goalie?' I asked, folding my arms determinedly. No way was I going in again. No one would look me in the eye. All lined up behind Dunner.

'Ah lads, come on, I'm shit in goal,' I said.

'You're shit at penos too,' Jasmine laughed, 'so it makes no difference.' The cheeky wagon.

'Youse owe me. Big time!' I grumbled as I made my way to goal. 'And no way am I feckin' in tomorrow.'

I got my position, bent my knees like I'd seen on the TV, trying to make myself look like I knew what I was doing. But no matter what I looked like, I was crap in goal. I couldn't catch, I couldn't block, and I most definitely couldn't do a long kick-out.

Jasmine was up first. Jasmine was better than the whole lot of us put together. She was better than anyone I knew. She played for the under-sixteen A team at our local club, the boys' team, even though she was only twelve. She grabbed fistfuls of her fizzing red hair and piled it quickly on top of her head, fastening it with a black elastic band.

'Jesus, Finn, your nose.'

'Yeah, Jasmine.' I could feel it running, but I wasn't wiping it to let her have free rein on goal.

'No seriously, Finn, it's pumping.'

I cupped a hand under my chin, which immediately filled with blood. Pools of it. I lifted the bottom of my shirt and pressed it hard against it.

'Here, Finn, use this,' Shane said, throwing his jumper, leaving a lopsided goalpost.

'It looks bad,' Dunner said.

The three were crowded around me now. Looking. Worried. I tried to laugh it off, but the blood kept coming. Jasmine ran to get me Ma.

That was sign number one.

Joe

Life just goes on. Sitting here at the front of Mr Murphy's English class, it's as if nothing has even happened. Murphy has gone for his five-minute fag break, Johnny Mitchell is piling spitballs torn from the back pages of *Macbeth*, empty biro shooter at the ready, and Phonsie Dunphy's blaring *Nevermind* through his portable Bluetooth speaker. Dunphy is such a pretentious bollox; he doesn't even know what *Nevermind* is, or stands for, and I'm pretty sure he can't name any member of Nirvana other than Kurt, if even that, but hipster code says one must love Nirvana. Fuck hipster bullshit.

They all turned up to the funeral, the teachers too, huddled together unable to conceal their fear of scumbag. Terrified that the cars they left in the unattended car park would be keyed or nicked. They eyed the bars on the church windows as they entered and huddled closer, knowing that no amount of holy water blessing was going to save them. You see, even as I'm here, in the same black crested blazer and pinstriped tie, the others can still smell the scholarship off me.

Look, the lads are all right really, and mostly they keep out of my way. I don't bother them, they don't bother me. Now everything sets my nerves on edge. Everything is raw and Dunphy's music is cracking my skull.

'Listen, Dunphy, would ya mind turning that off?' I ask, trying not to show I'm pissed off right. Dunphy acts as if he hasn't heard me, the prick. He's just put 'Smells Like Teen Spirit' on loop.

'Seriously, Phons, could ya please just turn it off?'

He smirks and turns the volume up. Playing air guitar to the drum riff. I get out of my seat and right into his face:

'Turn it the fuck off, Dunphy.' But Jesus, he just keeps on singing. I give him a push. Full force on his chest, and he's splayed on the ground and his lensless glasses are busted and my breathing is gone to fuck.

'You bloody well deserved that,' Johnny Mitchell shouts from the back to cheers from the others, but all I can think of is that despite my efforts, despite all that I've witnessed, I'm just like me Da.

/

'Joe, I really wish I didn't have to do this. You know that, right?' Mr Broderick says while taking out a booking slip. A yellow one. That's my second one this term, the second one since I started St Augustine's College just over four years ago.

He was one of the first to call, Mr Broderick was. As soon as he heard the news, he called round to the flat. Sat on our sofa and chatted with Ma. He brought round a lasagne, and Guinness stew, and a big box of biscuits, not once mentioning the state of the place, or the state of us. But here I am, in his office again, and he's still concerned. Always concerned. That I'm missing classes, that I'm causing fights, that his usual two-page *Irish Times* spread on inclusion and access and equality will be tainted by my bad news.

'One more yellow slip, son, and you're suspended. Do you understand, Joe?' he says, while using his Murano glass fountain pen to fill in my slip.

He is looking at me now, at his scholarship boy who is not meeting expectations.

'Do you want to talk to someone, Joe? A professional. I can organise it here in the school, if you'd like? It would be discreet. You could use my office.'

I'm not answering, or listening. Just looking past him and his antique walnut desk and his winged leather-backed chair, to the hall-of-fame pictures of past head teachers, Mr Broderick's standing out black and white and frameless in a sea of thick gilt and conceited posing.

'It's just that Ms Smith has told me you've stopped going to your portfolio classes,' he says.

'So is that another yellow slip, sir?' I ask, unable to conceal the crack in my voice. Betraying me.

'No, Joe. No, it's not that. It's just, we're all worried about you.' His hand is reaching out. For what – my hand, a fatherly shoulder-pat? I pull my arms in and tuck my hands firmly under my armpits. 'Look,' he continues, 'you need to start facing up to what has happened.' I keep my head down and pull my arms in tighter, folding myself away from him and what he has to say.

'I really do think you should talk to someone. You know I'm here, any time, and yes, I'm not an expert, but what I do know is that when grief comes knocking on your door, you have a choice, although it might not feel like it at the time, but I promise you, you do. Are you going to open that door and face it head on, or are you going to keep that door closed, try to lock it all out?' I can feel my mouth drying, my heart thumping, my hands sweating.

'Trust me, from experience, locking it out only makes it surge, makes it unbearable.' The tightening and fluttering at my throat is beginning to swell, but I am fixed, rooted to the chair, not able to move, or breathe, trying to block out what is being said, letting it whitewash right over me.

'I'm not pretending that I know what you are going through, and yes, you need time to process all that has happened, but you earned your place here, out of hundreds of applicants, not just because of your academic record, but because of who you are, your determination, your grit, and your art, Joe. You're talented. Really, really talented. Please don't give up on that.'

I run my thumb over the indented lump of hard skin on the middle finger of my left hand, forever stained with black ink and charcoal that no amount of scrubbing will remove.

'Will you at least go and talk to Ms Smith? To arrange some catch-up classes?' he says, holding my gaze. I hold it back.

'Yes, sir,' I say, with no intention of going near Ms Smith. She can keep her fucking concern too.

14

'All right so, Joe,' and he's standing to signal we're finished, and he's shaking my hand like an adult.

'I'm here, Joe. If you need me.' His hand is still shaking
mine. 'Any time, Joe, I mean it.' He gives it an extra-firm
squeeze and walks me to the door.

But he doesn't understand.

He doesn't see.

How can I draw any more, when it was all for him?

/

Johnny is waiting for me after school. He's usually on the
Dart southbound to his sea-fronted mansion by now. But
here he is, sitting on the top step waiting for me. I don't
want his pity.

'Hey,' he calls, scrambling to his feet, skipping down the
last few steps to catch up with me. 'Listen, I've been meaning to ask you . . .' He seems completely oblivious to the
fact that I'm ignoring him. I quicken my pace. He keeps up.

'I'm having a get-together at mine this Saturday. Will
you come?'

Is he having a laugh? I'm having flashbacks to Johnny's
eighteenth, his Ma cornering me to tell me she was doing
a brunch in The Shelbourne to aid 'my people', his Da telling me through billows of cigar smoke what a great young
man I was for trying to rise above my station, all the time
keeping his eyes fixed on me like a hovering security guard
in Penneys.

'The DJ starts at nine but cocktails are at eight,' he says.

Jaysus, a fucking cocktail party. Typical Augustine boys bollox. Taking my smirk as confirmation, he slaps my back in prep-boy companionship.

'Ah no, Johnny, I don't know now, I'm not really into all that Bloody Mary stuff.'

'Fuck Bloody Mary, and anyway, we're only serving gin-based cocktails,' he says. I look to see if he's joking. He's not, but his brace-straightened teeth are smiling at me like a mad yoke.

'Look, it's not really my thing.' Nothing is really my thing any more. I have to get away from him and his smiling face and his niceness. No one can be that fucking nice all of the time. But Johnny is.

'Come on, I'm not taking no for an answer, and Naoise is only dying to get back into you since last time, she hasn't stopped going on and on and . . . oh Christ, Joe, I didn't mean—' and his face is flushing and he's trying to cover up using *that* word. I laugh. Really laugh, feeling a little bit fucking normal again for the first time in ages.

'So, you'll come?' he asks, relieved that I'm returning back to myself, if even just a little.

'Sure, will see, yeah,' I say.

'Ah brilliant, Joe, brilliant,' he says, but he's lost eye contact now, and is scuffing the path with the top of his shoe.

'There's just one more thing,' he says, 'feel free to tell me to fuck off, right.' He's still not looking at me, a heat coming to his cheeks. 'It's just some of the guys were asking me to, you know, ask you,' and he takes a quick glance at me then, the heat of his awkwardness creeping further still, scorching me with the inevitability of what's coming. Not so fucking nice after all.

'To get ya some gear,' I say, throwing him his much-needed lifeline.

'Yes, that's it, thanks Joe,' he says, the smile coming back to his face, the heat draining out and transferring to me. 'You don't mind, do you? I was afraid you'd think,' and he lifts his two hands up either side of him, into some half-arsed shrug. Afraid I'd think what? That he was my friend, that he was different, that he was the only one about this place that looked at me and didn't see me Da.

'Yeah, it's a no,' I say, turning my back on him, the certainty of my position within the Augustine boys circle now well and truly confirmed.

'Oh, but you know you can name your price,' he says, trying to get back to the comfort of his warm comradeship. 'We're not looking for freebies or anything, in case that is what you were thinking, even get you a good mark-up for your trouble too. I promise.' He's waiting for me to answer, ignorant to the intensified shift between us.

'I said no, Johnny,' I say, and push my way through the crowd now gathered for after-school study, my back hunched, tensed towards him. He catches up, puts his hand on my arm.

'Hey, sorry, I didn't think you'd mind, honestly, it's not

a bother that you can't.' I turn to him, to see if he really is that clueless, but his face all open and friendly disarms me, makes me second-guess my anger.

'I just can't, OK,' I say and he nods OK back.

It's then that I feel her, two hands covering my eyes, turning my vision into a glow of hot pinks and reds, all 'Guess who,' said with a whisper of spearmint into my neck, her arms now around my shoulders, her lips with a kiss on my cheek, her quiet calm enveloping me. Her lovely still calm.

'Naoise,' I say, with the familiar flame of embarrassment. She moves beside me now, her bangled arm in around my waist, her fingers tickling at the side of me as they brush past. I'm afraid to budge, or say anything in case she moves away.

'Have you asked him yet,' she says to Johnny, and I feel myself tense; is that what she sees me as too, a mule for her and her rich buddies, her grapefruit scent now stinging at the raw exposed parts of me, the bits I didn't ever want her to see. Johnny notices, gives me a nudge and a smile.

'She means to the party,' he says and looks at me quizzically, pleadingly. I can feel her pulling me closer into her. I can't help but let it carry me, ease me into a grin. Johnny grins too.

'So, you'll come?' he asks, relieved that he's back on steady ground.

'Fuck it,' I say.

What's the worst that could happen?

Finn

Sat in Dr Flynn's office that first time and all I could smell was sick and antiseptic wipes.

'Vomiting bug epidemic,' Dr Flynn said, shrugging, as he inspected my nose with his gimpy pink shirt and fat-arsed jeans. He had just removed the third blood-filled cotton swab, more roughly this time, annoyed that the flow hadn't stopped.

'You'll just have to keep this up,' he said to Ma, showing her how to shove the cotton bud up far enough. 'It really should start to ease off soon.'

'What if it doesn't?' Ma wanted to know.

'Please, Mrs O'Reilly, I've already explained, there's not much else to do,' he said, passing her a jumbo pack of cotton swabs, a big buy-one-get-one-free sticker on the front. 'You just have to wait it out,' he said while standing to open the door. 'Nosebleeds are very common, Mrs O'Reilly, as I'm sure you know.' He pulled his phone out of his back pocket to check the time. I could feel the heat off Ma. She pushed back her chair, grabbed my hand and reefed me out the door.

'Don't forget to fix up with Sheila on your way out,' Dr Flynn called through his almost-closed door. 'Oh, and it's the after-hours rate,' he said, as the door clicked shut.

'After hours, me hoop,' Ma muttered, tightening her grip on me, walking straight past Sheila in her glass box.

'Mrs O'Reilly,' Sheila said. 'Oh Mrs O'Reilly, I think you forgot . . .' but Ma just kept walking. Ignoring her and dragging me with her.

'But Mrs O'Reilly—'

Ma swivelled, went right up close to the glass. Tapped it with her finger. Stared Sheila out of it. Sheila looked away first.

'You think I'm paying that jumped-up ponce to shove a cotton bud up his nose? You can tell Dr Flynn to fuck off.' And out the door we slammed.

Ma stayed in stony silence on the walk home, me practically running to keep up with her power strides. But I couldn't, keep up that is. My legs were throbbing. My bones were on fire.

'Ma, can we slow down.'

'Jaysus, Finn, it's only another ten minutes.'

'Ma, my legs are seriously banjaxed,' I said, and this time she stopped to look, and her face softened. A little. The hard lines around her mouth and eyes melting. A little.

'Did ya see the face on your one?' I said, trying to keep her soft.

She was nearly there.

'And the fat arse on Dr Flynn?' I said. and she exploded with laughter. Both of us breaking our holes at Dr Flynn. The eejit.

'Come on, we'll go for an ice cream, rest those legs of

yours,' Ma said, linking her arm in mine as we made our way towards the golden arches.

But those legs of mine. Those aching bones.

That was sign number two.

Joe

My phone vibrates on the coffee table. Sabine.

You comin round, Nan's made coddle.

Fuckin coddle, it's a bleedin heatwave.

Ha, I know, come on, we'll get a 99 after.

Sabine is on floor fifteen, top of the house, which is grand for her, but Nanny Gertie is pushing eighty and the lift is always fucked. And surprise surprise, cripple Ned is out, in his wheelchair, sunning himself.

'Howya, Ned.'

'All right, Joe,' Ned says, wheeling himself closer, getting ready for the gossip. Christ knows where he got the wheelchair; it wasn't from any doctor, that's for fucking sure.

'How's your Ma, Joe?' he asks, and he's practically wheeled onto my toe.

'Ah you know yourself, Ned, she's not getting out much these days.'

'Yeah, terrible, fucking terrible it is. I was only just saying there to Noeleen we haven't seen her in ages. Is she going back to the Tavern? You have the best craic with Annie, that's what we all say, and sure your one Tina can't pull pints for shite. She doesn't even tilt the glass, and she always uses the warm ones, straight out from the dishwasher so she does. Anyway, will ya tell her that we miss her about the place,' he says.

'Will do, Ned,' I say, and I try to squeeze myself past him, but he backs up, blocking the way.

'You know, I've been thinking, Joe, what happened there to young Finn, it's not natural, there's more to that, I tell you.'

Here we go again.

'It's the council, Joe. They're pumping something through the heating system. Poisoning our brains. You ever wondered why we can't control the heating? That's why, Joe. I'm telling you. Trying to flush us out, a bit of the auld Hitler cleansing shit going on.'

'Yeah, Ned, and Elvis lives over in Gandhi,' I say.

Ned and his fucking conspiracy theories.

'You can joke all you like, Joe, but I'm telling ya, I've started a letter to the council and everything—'

'Listen, Ned,' I cut him off. 'I really have to get on, Gertie has made a coddle.'

'A coddle? On the hottest day of the bleedin' year,' he says, laughing.

'Tell me about it,' I say, then I rap on Sabine's window.

'So she's made a coddle now, has she?' Ned says as Sabine opens the door.

'Fuck off, Ned,' she says and pulls me into a hug, the smell of boiled sausages and bacon stuck to her hair. I follow her through to the table, already set for three.

/

'Did ya not like it, Joe?' Gertie asks, looking at my half-finished bowl, the colourless sausages and potatoes floating around in its sea of vegetable soup.

'Nan, who the hell wants to be eating coddle in this heat?' Sabine says, laughing.

'That's enough from you, young lady. You can't just stop your meat and veg for a heatwave. You still need your sustenance. Get those hairs on your chest. Come on, Joe, don't you be letting me down now, eat up.'

I try an extra few spoonfuls for her benefit. She goes to the counter, fussing herself, buttering slices of Brennans Batch, cutting them in half and piling them onto the plate beside me. On top of the three already cut slices.

There's a photo on the windowsill, peeking out between all of Gertie's knick-knacks and Holy Marys, of the two of us. Me and Sabine, that is, on the first day of school. Me, dark and sulking; her, freckled and red-ribboned plaits and a grin so wide it nearly cracks her face. Arms around each other, leaning against the gate of St Brendan's National School towering above us all steel and barbed.

I can see that gate from our flat, the messing and scraps of school-time madness, the laughs and whoops from Finn and his mates, as they swung out of the bicycle racks, Principal Kelly giving a good auld *get out of it* roar.

'Nan, we're going for a ninety-nine, do ya want us to bring anything in?' Sabine asks while clearing the plates, piling them into the sink. I give her a hand.

'Are you just going to leave them like that?' Gertie says, nodding at the precarious tower.

'Ah Nan, look, we have to get out of here before we're boiled alive,' she says, giving Gertie a big hug from behind and a kiss on the cheek. 'Leave them there, and we'll clean up when we're back. Promise,' Sabine says, her arms still tight around her.

'All right so, love,' Gertie says. 'Oh, and will you pick us up a TV guide, I want to see who is on the *Late Late* tonight.'

'Ah Nan, I can just look that up for you on me phone,' Sabine says, reaching for her back pocket.

'Jesus, Mary and Joseph, no. I want to read it like a normal human being, thank you very much. Sure, don't I like doing the crossword, reading the gossip. Now go get my purse, there's a good girl.'

Sabine retrieves it from under the green floral footstool, the one perched beside the good chair, and hands it to her. Gertie takes out a crumpled fiver and folds it into Sabine's hand. 'The ninety-nines are on me, love,' she says.

We make our way across The Yard, to between Gandhi and Mandela, where the ice-cream van usually camps on a scorcher. We join the queue of worn-out Mas and sticky-faced toddlers and young lads counting their coppers.

'Here, mister, you wouldn't have twenty cent, would ya?' a freshly peeling face asks, hand over his eyes, shielding. I rummage around my faded jeans pocket and flick him a fifty. 'Ah nice one, thanks,' he says, as he and his mates start recalculating what they can get with their extra thirty cent. Meanies or Hubba Bubba?

We lick our ninety-nines on the wall of the abandoned shopping centre, the hub of the towers that never actually got occupied in the first place. You couldn't even buy a loaf of bread in this fucking place, had to hoof it all the way into town for that, a good twenty minutes' walk away.

'Tell your Ma I saved your life.' It's Carthy, taking a break from his booming business by the looks of it, pushing Sabine from behind, off the wall, and pulling her back again, into him, his hands on her waist.

Sabine elbows him in the ribs. 'Get the fuck, Carthy.' He just pulls her tighter.

'She said, get the fuck,' I say, standing, ready to burst him.

'Relax the fucking cacks, man,' he says, raising his hands, hawking a glob of green phlegm over Sabine's shoulder onto the path in front of her. 'I'm only having a laugh. Isn't that right, Sabine,' he whispers into her neck, and she's hunched now, arms crossed over herself, each hand at either side of her neck.

'She said, get the fuck,' I say again, and wedge my body between them.

'All right, all right,' he says, and he moves away, towards the Tavern, stained boxers on show over his bagging jeans. 'She's nothing but a frigid cock-tease anyway.' And he's footing it, giving sneaky smirks over his shoulder.

'How long has he been doing that?' I ask, barely able to keep the fire out. 'Sabine, seriously, what the fuck is the story there?' She leans into me. Sabine. Who never leans on anyone. Who is strong as fuck. Who never gives a shit what people say or think of her.

'Leave it, Joe,' she says.

'Did something happen?' I ask, and she doesn't answer, she just ups and heads back towards the flat.

Finn

Da was there when we got home. Sitting on the couch between a crust-filled Domino's box and three crushed cans of Dutchie. I wonder did he do shotgun with the cans. He showed me how with a can of Fanta once, piercing a hole in its side and getting me to put my mouth on it while he pulled the tab. I could still feel the sticky burn of bubbles in my nose three days later. I inspected the cans from where I stood, but I couldn't see any holes.

He had his sleeves rolled up, Da did, and I could just about see his favourite tattoo. The one he got for Ma on her birthday, the Annie one, written in big black swirling letters with a star over the 'i'. He said he liked everyone to know that Ma belonged to him, but especially Ma. He said he liked her to have that reminder most of all.

I can't wait to get a tattoo. Dunner's older brother Anto does them. He nicked a load of stuff from some tattoo place in town and now he does them round his flat for half price. Dunner told me he learned how to do them from YouTube. Joe said he hasn't a clue and his tattoos all look like shite, but Dunner said Anto will give us one when we're fourteen, and no way am I going to waste it on a girl's name, not even Ma's.

'Where were youse?' Da asked, not lifting his eyes from *The Chase* blasting through the flat-screen.

'The doctor,' Ma answered, nodding at my bedroom door, pushing me in its direction, but I wanted to sit with Da and watch *The Chase*. I pushed the empty cans to the ground and scooched in beside him.

'The doctor?' Da said. 'Which one did you go to? I hope it wasn't that bollox in the health centre, he's a nosy bastard, him. Always poking around in our business.'

'No, we went to your man Flynn up there on Sheriff Street,' Ma said, but Da didn't answer back, he just kept watching *The Chase*.

'Ha, did you see that, Finney boy. She's just pressed the wrong button, the geebag. It's A. You should have pressed A, you dopey bitch.' But as he nudged me with his elbow, he took in my bloody shirt and drenched cotton swabs.

'Who the fuck busted you?' he asked.

'No one, Da, it's a nosebleed.'

'What? A fucking nosebleed?' He turned to look at Ma now. 'You took him to the doctor for a poxy nosebleed. I've fucking told you before, Annie, you're going to turn him into a complete bleedin' sissy.' He nudged me with his elbow again, harder this time, in the ribs. I didn't let on that it hurt.

'Here, Da, your one is after getting it wrong again,' I said, trying to get him back. But he'd already gone and was headed towards Ma. Ma kept her back to the counter. Like always.

'Who'd you say you went to?' he asked, leaning his hand on the counter behind her.

'Dr Flynn,' said Ma, barely moving.

'Flynn,' Da said. 'You mean that posh pillock. How much did that set me back?' And he pressed his hand hard on hers.

'Nothing, Da,' I said. 'It cost us nothing. We didn't pay, isn't that right, Ma?' But I've said the wrong thing. I can see it in Ma's face.

'Nothing.' His foot was on hers now. 'Are you making a fucking charity case out of us?'

'Finn, to your room. Now,' Ma ordered.

'That's right, send your little Mammy's boy to his room, God forbid he sees what a real man must do to get some fucking respect,' he said, pushing right up against Ma, his foot still on her foot, his hand still on her hand, and all I could think of is how Granda used to get me and Joe to stand on his feet and hold his hands while he danced us around the kitchen. I don't think Da wanted to dance.

'Finn,' Ma pleaded.

I got up and ran to my room. Joe was there on the bottom bunk, headphones in, and scratching on his sketchpad. I climbed the ladder and faced the wall, still studded with Liverpool stickers and cinema stubs. The mattress lifted twice, kicked from under me.

'You all right, bud?' Joe asked, his face peering over the side of the steel rail. 'Can I come up, yeah?' And he hopped up beside me without waiting for my answer. He placed a headphone in my ear and one in his own and turned up the volume, Thin Lizzy's 'Sarah'.

'I've made you another one,' he said, 'to add to the

collection,' and out from the centre of his sketchpad was Principal Kelly in a nappy, sucking his thumb, and I laughed my feckin' head off. I reached under my pillow and pulled out the Sellotape and taped it up with the rest. Just above my head where I could see it.

'Will you do Mrs O'Sullivan next?' I asked.

'Yeah,' Joe said, and he got a fresh page and his black pen and turned the volume up on Thin Lizzy.

'Will you make sure it's a nice one. I can show her then,' I said.

'Yeah, Finn, I'll do a nice one,' he said, and I concentrated on Joe's hand and the lyrics of 'Sarah'.

Joe

I can't get sight of Sabine, and I can't risk going back to her flat in case she's not there and I land her in it. I ring her. Again. No pick-up.

You back at yours?

Online

Just let me know you're all right.

Typing

I wait. Keep checking for her response, turn up the screen brightness so I can see, so I won't miss it.

Online

Fuck sake, Sabine.

Look, call up to us after, yeah?

Two grey ticks coloured blue. At least I know she's seen it.

I think about going to the Tavern, finding fuckface Carthy, putting a bit of O'Reilly pressure on, the shit. But that's what Da would do. That's what Da would want me to do. Fuck Da.

I walk around to the back of the flats, and head towards Captains Hill, the only bit of green in this sea of concrete and steel, broken glass and destruction. I climb to the top, up and over, and there she is. Feet stretched out in front of her.

'How did ya know I'd be here?' she says, puffing smoke rings high above her head, one after the other, the reek of smoke tinged with menthol lingering, no chance of evaporation in this dead heat.

I didn't.

Me and Sabine have been coming here since we were kids. All the kids come here. The hill, that is. You can roll down it on your own, all tucked in like a cannonball, or on your skates or your bike or Gertie's wooden canteen tray when it snowed. This is where we had the craic. Where Finn had the craic.

'Go on, give us a drag,' I say, and add a few rings of my own, mine not as polished or round as hers. 'Jaysus, Sabine, the state of those menthol yokes.'

'Go get your own so, ya fucking scab,' she says, pulling it back off me with a laugh, the old Sabine back, but shadowed. Shaded by fucking Carthy.

I don't say anything, I just sit close, shoulders touching, letting her lean in, alternating menthol inhalations with her diminishing fag butt.

'Look, Joe, I don't want to get into it,' she says, filling the silence.

'Has he done anything?' I ask. It's all I want to know. All I need to know. 'Sabine, has he?'

She begins to scrape at the flecks of green polish covering her chewed, ragged nails. 'Not yet,' she says, and takes a fresh fag out of the pack, lights it off the stub in her mouth, sucks hard till it ignites, then flicks the old one to the ground, stubbing it quickly off the sole of her worn red Converse.

'Not yet?' I ask, not able to keep it level. I dig my nails into the palm of my hand and hope it leaves a mark. 'What the fuck is that even supposed to mean, Sabine?' I dig harder.

'It means not yet,' she says, uncurling my fingers, lacing hers through mine and breathing with me, in and out until our breath returns to normal and we sit holding hands, watching the young ones race up and down Captains Hill in a variety of contraptions.

'It's Nanny,' she says after a while, taking her hand back, linking her fingers together around her dimpled knees, hugging them close. 'She went to Murphy for a loan.'

'Ah fuck. Sabine, why didn't you say anything?' She gives a quick glance, but continues on.

'I was applying for a spot, on that make-up course in town, you know the one I was on about, the one that does the special-effects stuff and everything. It's the best. Well, one of the best you can get here anyways. But the application was €250. You were guaranteed it back if you got a place. There were special scholarship spots and all.' She stops and starts plucking at clumps of grass underneath her.

'I didn't get a spot.'

I pull her in close, put my chin on her head and wrap my arms around tight. How did I not see this? How did I not know?

'And Carthy?'

She pushes herself away, back to picking the grass.

'He's collecting.'

No, there's no way. Carthy? Who in sixth class begged Sabine to take the blame for leaving an eggy sandwich in Ms McNamara's desk, right before midterm, who always needed me with him when Josie's pitbull was about The Yard, and now Dessie is entrusting him with the implementation of his threats, of getting results? Sure, who in their fuck would be afraid of him? They all rip the piss – Dessie, Da, I've heard them at it, at the flat. He's just a scrawny lick-arsed runner to them.

'They want me to sell,' she says, gulping at the extra breath in her, 'to clear the debt, and fuck, Nan,' she squeezes my hand, 'if she knew I was getting involved in something that stole Ma from us, that I could put that damage and hurt on someone else . . .'

'Sabine. No. There is no way he's collecting for Murphy. No fucking way. There's something else going on here.' I get up. 'Why didn't you tell me?' I ask again.

'Tell you,' she says. 'How the fuck could I tell you?' She's looking at me. Raging. 'You'd forgotten I'd even applied. Never even asked me about it. You hardly call round. You never phone. It's been four months, Joe. Four fucking months. You can't just . . .'

'Can't just what, Sabine?' I let out a harsh, rough laugh. I can't even help it. I still see him everywhere. The scribbles in the stairwell, the bench on The Yard; the place is filled with him. Here. Him flying down this hill. I get my two palms and press them hard into my sockets, trying to wipe the heat and the pain away, the scorch of anger pouring out of me. Always. Fucking. Pouring.

'Joe,' she says, reaching out for me as I stand. 'Joe,' she says again, trying to make contact, trying to pull me in as I walk away.

'Where are you going?' she calls after me.

'The Tavern.'

'Why?'

I ignore her.

'Why, Joe?' she says, louder this time.

'For a fucking drink, Sabine.' And I leave her, standing on Captains Hill, discarded fag butts at her feet.

Finn

'Right, there's the bell,' Mrs O'Sullivan said. 'Lunches out. Quickly.' She set the ten-minute timer on the interactive whiteboard.

I reached into my bag and pulled out my lunchbox. Sitting there, right on top of my digestive jam sandwiches, was Joe's Post-it.

'Who did he do for you this time?' Jasmine asked, leaning in to get a good gawk.

'Batman,' we said together.

Mrs O'Sullivan came down to see too.

'Ah, the Caped Crusader,' she said, then got the scrapbook from the reading corner and glued the Post-it in with Pritt Stick. The scrapbook was nearly full now. Full of Joe's Post-it sketches, signed *Just Joe* in the bottom right-hand corner. Mrs O'Sullivan said she had every intention of showing it off when Joe was a famous artist.

'Will ya give us a bit of that?' Jasmine asked, as I opened the wrapper of my Fruit Winder. I unravelled it to full length, bit it in half and catapulted her half over. I pushed up my sleeves and wrapped mine around my wrist.

'Saving it for later,' I told her. She had hers already eaten.

The whiteboard timer flashed ten seconds.

'I'll get the ball,' Jasmine shouted, and I snapped closed

my lunchbox and flung it on the floor.

'Lunchboxes in school bags, please,' Mrs O'Sullivan said, looking straight at me. I tugged on the zip of my bag, trying to yank it open, trying not to miss a second of big break.

'Ah Miss, it's stuck,' I said, as the rest of the class ran out the door with the bell.

'Bring it here, Finn,' she said, and took the bag from me and had it open just like that. Using her famous elbow grease.

'It's the extra material. See here, Finn, the one covering the zip, you need to keep that away from it.' I just wanted my bag back and to get out with the rest. I reached my hand out to get it from her, but she just held it outstretched and stared at my arms.

'Where did you get those, Finn?' she asked, pointing to the bruises running up and down both arms.

'Just from tag, Miss, in yard earlier.'

'From today?'

'Yeah.'

'Finn, they look older. Are you sure it was from today?'

'Yeah, definitely, Miss, they weren't there this morning, anyway.' I wished she would just let me go already.

'It must have been rough. I've told the class before about rough play on yard. Do I need to consult Mr Kelly?'

'No, Miss, honestly, it wasn't rough, just the usual tag.'

I'd a few under my knees too, from swinging on the steel bicycle rack just behind the main school gate, but I wasn't going to tell Mrs O'Sullivan that. I didn't want a trip to Principal Kelly's office or worse, him visiting the class.

'Can I go now, Miss?' I asked. I'd wasted about five minutes already and all the best spots would be taken. I'd be left as referee again.

'Yes, Finn, off you go,' she said, and took out her notebook, the one she leaves in the top drawer, the locked one, and wrote something down. I began to run towards the class door.

'Finn, your lunchbox.' I rammed it into my bag, zipped it up and ran to find Jasmine, Dunner and Shane.

Six minutes late.

I bet I'm the feckin' referee.

Joe

Fat Mick is on the door, all black trousers and fake leather jacket and the sweat only pumping off him. Not so much a bouncer as a beady-eyed watcher, a snitch for Murphy's gang, to give a heads up if anyone who didn't know their place was about. And he'd put you in your place all right, if it was needed. Right into the A & E waiting room, all busted to shite.

He's positioned just how he likes it, in the space of the one opened double door, wedged in tight, no way of taking a quick peek in, bars on the windows and Fat Mick at the door, no quick getaway either.

He stands aside when he sees me coming, at least he has the cop for that.

'Ah howya, head,' he says, smiling as I cross his threshold. I'm not in the mood for chewing the fat.

'We're all missing Annie about the place. Is she coming back to us any time soon?' He places his hand on my shoulder, giving it a staccato double pat, knuckles freshly cracked and blooming.

'Could ya just leave it to fuck, Mick, yeah,' I say, and I walk on past him, to the chaos that is the Tavern.

The place is hopping; Thursday is dole day and everyone is sloshing the cash, buying the rounds, whooping it up. Any excuse is the fucking motto here. The two-piece band, Abba-Salutely, are crammed into the corner, playing all those ABBA hit wonders for the auld ones, bet into their leopard prints, the sax solo unbearably loud, filling the air around us.

The carpet has a firm stick to it as I make my way to the bar, and the place is filled with smoke, stinging my eyes, the makeshift smoking area just outside the propped-open fire escape doing nothing to prevent the smoke from smothering this poxy place.

The lads, the old gang, are about the pool table. Redzer and Spud and Gimpy. The eyes are hanging out of their heads, euro coins stacked on the pool-table ledge, even though no one else ever bothers with a game. It is always left to the lads.

'Well, would you look at who's decided to grace us with his presence,' Redzer calls, the drink giving him a little Dutch courage.

'All right, Joe,' Gimpy says, giving us a nod.

Redzer gives him a thump. 'What are ya talking to that prick for, too good for us now, so he is, up in his posh private school, all posh and fucking private,' he spits, barely able to stand.

'Jaysus tonight,' Spud says. 'Just get on with the game, yeah.'

Redzer, eyes still on me, stumbles across the floor, skidding into the jacks. 'I'm taking a slash,' he says, 'but I'll be back to say me piece.' Yeah, in his hole he will. All trousers and no balls, him.

I remember it was always us around that table, from younger than Finn, all of us, and Carthy, and the Mas and Das throwing over a big box of Tayto and bottles of red lemonade, and we'd spend hours playing pool, playing darts, stealing change left on the counter, and me and Carthy pulling out the band's sound system, hiding their leads when they were out getting the rest of their gear, and the roars and shouts out of them when they came back, and me and Carthy busting our holes laughing, and I still remember his face, Carthy, when I told him I'd got the scholarship, how I wouldn't be going to the local VEC after all, how Ma had finally persuaded Da, after weeks of begging, and how it all had made a liar out of me.

I take a stool at the bar. I have to go in the middle – the one in the corner, the one for skulking, is already taken. I can see straight behind the bar here, straight into Dessie Murphy's snug. His eyes lock on mine as I take my seat.

'A Guinness, Pat, when you're ready.' He gets a glass, pulling it, the look of resentment on his face with every drop. His Da owns a pub in Spain but makes him look after the family business here. He wants to be sunning it in the Costa del Sol, not getting sweaty burnt fuckers drinks in Dublin.

'Your Ma about?' he asks, leaving the pint to rest.

I don't answer. But I know what he's getting at, the bollox.

'She's rightly left me fucked, you know? Will you tell her that from me. Fucking fucked, big time.' He rants away as I sit waiting for my pint.

'Can I not just drink me pint, Pat? Can you not even let me do that, in a bit of bleedin' peace, like?'

'Listen, you little fuck, I don't even have to serve you,' he says, tapping at his *Management Reserves the Right* sign taking pride of place beside his triple-X barmaids postcards. 'Not to mention you're underage, to fucking boot. Tell her if she's not back by the end of next week, she can fuck off with herself. I've a load of young ones only dying to work here, bleedin' begging me so they are, you should see the pile of CVs I have back at the gaff,' he says, tapping the bar with his beer mat.

This is why I hate the middle seat. You always get landed in the chats with fucking Pat.

'Ah for fuck's sake, he's at it again,' Pat says, and he's out from behind the bar and over to Ned, stuck in the door of the jacks with his chair.

'This isn't accessible, Pat, I should have the safety officer out to ya,' Ned says, repeatedly bashing his chair off the frame of the door.

'Ned, you're not even a bleedin' cripple, would ya just get out of the chair and into the jacks and we'll say no more a-fucking-about it.'

'It's discrimination, that's what it is. Bleedin' discrimina-tion,' says Ned, still trying to jam his way in, bits of the frame starting to splinter in jagged edges around him. He'd want to watch it or he'd get a splinter in the mick. No laugh-ing matter, that.

'You're going to have to carry me in, Pat,' Ned says,

stretching out his two arms, half lifting himself out of the chair.

'Carry you in, get the fuck,' says Pat, who starts trying to dump Ned out of the chair, Ned hanging on for dear life, his heels dug in in front of him, keeping him grounded.

I reach behind the bar, grab my pint, and top it with a flick of the pump in front of me. I rub my thumb down the length of the glass and take a long sip. Only one pint, mind you, enough to dull but not take control.

The snug is filling up now. Dessie lording it over the lot of them. He has them all eating out of the palm of his hand, not daring to knock the hand that feeds them.

It's hard to separate the memories from the capabilities of the man that is Dessie 'The Badger' Murphy. Myself and Finn used to love when Dessie would call. A big bag of jelly babies and a packet of Kimberley flung onto the table in front of us.

'Get that into ya, Jacinta,' he'd say, laughing, tearing open the packet and firing biscuits at you, one after the other. He never brought his kids, though, or we never went to his. Him always on his own, to our flat, and he'd give us a fiver after a while, to get us the fuck out, to let him and Da have the chats. Here he is in the snug, still having the chats with the right sort of lads.

They've tried to take him down, the Guards that is. They have even planted some of their own, trying to win the glory and the fame and the promotions that bringing down The Badger, head of the infamous Townies gang, would inevitably bring. But he has a knack for sniffing them out. Sniffing out anyone who doesn't belong, who doesn't know what side their bread is buttered. And he always lets them know it, slowly but surely. Always fucking slowly.

Dessie likes to think that he got his nickname from his fearless but vicious tendencies. But the head on him, all jet black set with a shock of white, speaks the truth, the whole truth and nothing but the truth. It's that simple.

I sit drinking my pint and let it warm me, fill me, hoping that the dullness will start soon, wishing I could just sit here and down pint after pint and let everything wash over me. Like Ma. Pass out to a blackness that holds no memory.

I spy Carthy now, and the grip on my pint tightens. He's mooching around the edge of the snug, trying to get a foothold. He's just hovering though, not in, not out. Slyly clinging to the edge. You can't just join the Townies, no matter how much you want in. You are invited, head-hunted, initiated. You need to have a fucking purpose. And each purpose is unique. No double-jobbing here. Only Townies get a seat at the snug table. Carthy is nowhere near that table, but Murphy is letting him lurk, and there is something in that.

He's there now, scratching his chest, takes out a small black phone from inside his jacket, not the obvious one protruding from the back pocket of his jeans. Looks around, and fires a quick text and zips it back in. Quickly.

A whoosh of warm air hits my back as Sabine enters.

'For paying customers only,' Pat says, his determined hands still pushing and pulling out of Ned's chair.

'Ah I love you too, Pat,' Sabine calls back, pulling up a stool beside me.

'Look, Sabine, I'm sorry, yeah?' I say.

'Forget it,' she says. 'Let's just forget it, yeah?'

That suits me. She reaches over and grabs my pint, downing the rest of it. I leave her to it. I look out the fire escape, and Carthy is in the middle of the lads now, having left the snug, and he's in a jock, off his head, laughing and joking and pulling at the tip of his mickey, and Murphy is looking on. Silently.

Finn

There was a knock on the door. I took a peek out the bedroom window: it was Mrs O'Sullivan. What was she doing here at the flat? Had she found out about the bicycle rack? Was it because I couldn't find my copy for last night's maths homework? But sure, Joe gave me a sheet of his foolscap, and I still got it done. She was mad into her copies and her red-penned margins and her one-number-per-box rules, so it probably was that. Maybe.

I opened my door a crack and looked out. There was a knack to spying in this place. The bedroom door had always been too fat to close properly, so that was one thing in your favour, and if you just opened it a little more, no one had a clue what you were at. You needed to stand the far side though, just behind it, so if someone did look over, they wouldn't see you peeking. I learned that when Da saw me once when he was having a meeting with The Badger. He slammed it on my fingers for being a sneaky little bastard, so I didn't do it that way again.

'Sorry to bother you, Mrs O'Reilly. Would you mind if I came in for a bit?'

I could see Ma's back, not moving, blocking the door.

'I promise I won't be long – just a quick chat about Finn is all,' she said.

'Finn? What's this all about? Could this not be done at the school?'

'If I could just come in, it'll only take a minute. I saw Mr O'Reilly hop on the bus there, heading into town, so I'd say he'll be a while.'

'What has that to do with anything?' Ma asked, her hand gripping the door. Making her block stronger.

'Nothing, Mrs O'Reilly, but it means we probably won't be interrupted is all.' She waited, not saying anything else.

Ma stood aside and let her in. Just about. Not asking her for tea, or clearing a space on the couch, or asking me to knock into Josie for the good biscuits.

'Well, what's going on?' Ma asked again, folding her arms tight across her chest, still blocking.

'I'm just a little concerned about Finn,' she said.

'What do you mean? Has he done something? It wouldn't be like him now if he has. He's a good boy, our Finn, so he is.'

'No, he's not in any trouble, not like that anyway. I was just wondering if everything is all right here,' she said. 'You know, with Mr O'Reilly?'

'Listen, I don't know what this is all about, Miss, but lurking around outside, waiting till Frank has left, asking me personal questions . . . so I'm asking again, what the fuck is going on?' And her hand was out, reaching for the latch of the door. Ready to shut her out.

'I'm sorry, I don't mean to pry. It's just I noticed some marks on Finn today, lots of them, big dark bruises, all over his arms. He said he got them from yard, chasing, but Mrs O'Reilly, I just don't believe him.'

'So you're calling my Finn a liar?'

'No, of course not, but I was wondering why he would lie, if he is.'

'What are you trying to get at, Miss?'

'Look, I didn't do this through the official means, yet. I know where that can lead. But I will if I have to, understand? I just wanted to check if you might know where the bruises came from first.'

'All up his arms, you say?'

'Yes, Mrs O'Reilly, literally covered. There is no way he would have gotten them from a game of tag like he says.' Ma's hand dropped from the latch, she was making her way towards my room.

'Finn,' Ma called, 'would you come out here for a minute, love?' I stepped back from my spying spot, made a show of getting up from the bed, not letting on that I'd been hid behind the door, being a sneaky little bastard.

'Love,' Ma said, 'Mrs O'Sullivan here is a bit worried about the marks on your arm. Would ya mind showing us?' I rolled up my sleeves to let them get a look. They were darker now, all a mash of yellow and purple, and covered both arms.

'Jesus, Finn, what the fuck happened? Who did that to you?' Ma asked.

'No one, it was from tag, in school today.'

'Finn, no one gets bruises like that from tag. When did

it happen?' Ma held on to both my hands and looked me straight in the eyes. 'You can tell me, love, no matter who it was, you can tell me.'

'You're not in any trouble, pet,' Mrs O'Sullivan added.

'It was just from playing, Ma, honest,' I said, holding her gaze.

'Have you any more?'

I hesitated.

'Finn.' She held my hands a little tighter.

'OK. Yeah. I have some on the backs of my legs too, from hanging off the bicycle racks at school.' I took a quick look at Mrs O'Sullivan. She nodded and gave a little smile. Maybe she wouldn't rat me out to Kelly after all.

'Can I see?' Ma asked.

I rolled up the bottom of my trousers as far as they would go.

'Jesus, love, they're all up the back of your legs too. Are you sure that's how you got them? Please, Finn. Just make sure you're being honest with me. Promise me, love.'

'I swear, Ma, that's how I got them.' I couldn't remember how I got bruises before. I didn't even think these were bad. Yeah, they were big, and colourful, and a bit mental looking, but they were only feckin' bruises. I didn't break my arms or legs or anything like that.

'Right, love, you can go back to your room. I just want to chat to Mrs O'Sullivan a bit longer.' I went back to my hiding place, behind the door.

'I swear to you, he's never laid a hand on him, and yeah,

I know you think I'd cover for him, but there is no fucking way I would let him ever touch the boys. Either of them. I would rather let him kill me than that.'

'I know, Mrs O'Reilly, but you can see why I had to check.'

'What do you think it means? If he is telling the truth, sure no one should be getting bruises like that from what he's telling us.'

'I don't know, Mrs O'Reilly, I really don't.'

I still didn't get what the big deal was. They didn't even hurt. They were just a few bruises. What the hell did bruises ever do to anyone?

Joe

Ma is at the toaster when I get in, placing two Birds Eye waffles in its slot, heating some beans on the hob, kettle boiling at her side.

'Ah love, you're back,' she says, quickly rushing to tie the overflowing bin bag, all jingle-jangled with her empties.

'I wanted to have it ready, for when you came in, like.' She goes to give me a hug, and a kiss on the cheek, but it's all stiff and awkward and not like Ma. Not the way it was or is supposed to be. At least when there was hope we could cling to that, but once that left us, we could cling to nothing, not even each other.

'Ah don't be worrying, Ma, you sit down and I'll finish this up,' I say, and we're skirting around each other and the form of Him that is constantly wedged between us, still so fresh and unbearable, making us keep our distance.

'Jesus no, love, go on and sit down, I'll bring it over,' she says, stirring away at the beans with the wooden spoon that used to redden our arses when we got out of line. *Fucking discipline, Annie,* Da used to say, showing her how to use the full force of it, making sure she'd be doing it right.

'Pat was asking for ya, Ma,' I say.

'Ah go away to shite, asking for me or asking where I've been?'

'It might be good for ya, to get back out of the flat again, you've always loved it down at the Tavern,' I say. It's true. It was where Ma shone. She had a way with her. She made everyone feel better about themselves, especially the under-dog. She could handle any scrap inside too, and rarely had to resort to calling Fat Mick.

'We'll see, love,' she says, a bit of the forced cheer slipping out of view. She places the plate of grub in front of me, with a steaming mug of tea, and then stands hovering, not sure what to do, not sure how to reach out to me, or check how I am, or see how I'm feeling or coping. *I'm not, Ma*, I want to scream. *I'm the same as you. Crumbling.* But I don't say any of these things. I keep it bottled in, all screwed up tight, like always.

'You not having any, Ma, no?'

'Ah you're grand, love,' she says, and goes over to the couch, flicks on the TV, filling the silence, suppressing the golden opportunities.

'Looks good, Ma, thanks,' I say, with no response, at the table on my own, Finn's communion photo in my direct eyeline, smiling at me through his hand-me-down suit, completely oblivious to what would happen to him, to what he would cause.

'Oh, I meant to ask ya,' she says, pressing mute on the remote and twisting herself awkwardly to face me. 'Is Sabine doing all right?' I put the fork down, wondering what she's heard. 'It's just, I saw her there earlier, crossing The Yard, she's just not looking right, not herself, you know?' It's a long time since Ma's noticed anything, let alone something being off.

'Ah yeah, she's grand, didn't get a course she was after, feeling a bit sorry for herself, that's all.'

'If you say so,' she says, deceiving her never coming easy. 'Maybe ask her around, it's been ages, yeah,' she says, turning back to the TV, and to the comfort of not having to look too closely at me.

/

I raise my fist to knock, wanting to make a statement, a side-fisted sound always more menacing than a knuckle, so I'm told, but the door is already half open, fuck it anyway, not getting myself off to a good start. I prowl myself through it instead, thinking a fright will do the menacing for me, which only gets swallowed by the noise of the young ones killing each other about the place so I'm back to square one.

I'm behind him now; the threat of me is ever diminishing with each unrecognisable minute. He has the toddler on his hip, who is contentedly chewing at the teat of his bottle of Ribena, gurgling in delight as he manages to pull a bit of rubber away, allowing a gush of purple liquid to escape into the back of his throat and dribble down his chin, a big exaggerated gasp on him to show his enjoyment, David laughing at him while globbing luminous orange spaghetti hoops into bowls, freshly pinged from the microwave.

'Grub's up,' he shouts, his back still to me, the rest of the Carthy clan happily ignoring his request, Mary Louise's eyes fixed solidly to the screen of her phone, her thumb scrolling aimlessly, and Patrick and Shane tearing strips out of each other at her feet. There's the clammy claustrophobic look about the place that's always been there, crusted-on plates, half-filled mugs, empty wrappers and packaging cluttering the surfaces, the floors, and the syrupy, claggy smell of growing mould.

He places the toddler down and grabs a bowl for himself, turning as he's blowing on the spoon, dropping it straight back down on seeing me.

'All right, Sir Joe, to what do we owe this pleasure.' He takes a theatrical bow, rolling his arm out in front of him, taking a dig at me and my pedestal he so happily likes to highlight.

The toddler makes his way to me, pulling at the leg of my jeans with his freshly sticky hands, bouncing up and down on the toes of his bare feet, signalling for me to pick him up, which I do, clasping my grip under his armpits, him wriggling with the tickle of it, and woosha him up and down over my head, repeatedly, the husked rasped laughter of him getting louder and more excitable with each lift, running away delighted and breathless when I place him down again. I catch Carthy's eye then, him shifting a little, not sure where he stands with me.

'How long has it been this time,' I ask, despite myself. He continues to look at me like that, not quite believing that I'm here at all, and if he can trust me, and I can see the hesitation of the answer on his lips, can see it in his eyes, the weighing up of his decision to let me in again.

'Two weeks,' he says, 'but she's getting clean this time,' and we both give a laugh at that, knowing full well the story of Mrs Carthy's impromptu rehab sessions.

'Look, how much does she owe, Sabine,' I say, cutting to the chase.

'Ah so it's like that,' he says, the smirk firmly back in place.

'Just fucking tell us, yeah.'

'Six hundred, even-stevens.'

'Fuck off, sure Gertie only took two fifty.'

'Don't shoot the messenger,' and his hands are up in front of him, that fuck of a smile still plastering his face.

'I'll get it to ya,' I say.

'Will ya now.'

'Yeah, I will.'

'And how exactly are ya going to do that,' he says.

'None of your fucking business,' I say, slamming my fist on the counter in front. The toddler starts crying at the crash of it; Mary Louise picks him up, throwing me a filthy look as she carries him into the bedroom.

'Here we go again, Saint fucking Joe,' Carthy says, coming in close. 'Get your head out of your arse for even one second and look the fuck around,' he continues, his breath catching on a laugh. 'There is only one way you'll be getting that debt paid,' he says, 'and we all fucking know it.'

He picks up his bowl again then, starts shovelling the hoops into him, the sauce all dripping down his T-shirt.

/

I wait until Ma goes to bed, and leave an extra half an hour to be sure she's out for the count, although I'm not sure she'd be all that bothered, hearing me leave that is, the fight is just gone from her, too consumed by everything else to leave any space for worry or concern about me.

It's always worse in the dark. The shadows. The echoing noises of misery. The smells smothering you from all angles. The fear of not knowing what you're going to meet on the stairwell. Around that next corner. And I'm always brought back to when the electricity would trip, and Da would make me go down to the basement, to its sea of wires and scuttles of rats, as I'd edge myself along the length of its walls, with the torch from under the sink white-knuckle gripped in one hand, the handle of the brush in the other, ready to reset our switch, flicking it back into place.

It's still the same. The static shock of the place at night. Lads kicking the shite out of each other up and down the stairways. Drunken laughs, and shouts, and smacks bouncing off the bare walls, filling each and every space. The lights of The Yard still stoned dark, the glass of the bulbs long since shattered, and the methadone-withdrawn faces haunting the perimeter with their hollowed-out eyes, debating whether to fix it, looking hungrily at those already in the zone.

Carthy is there, like I knew he would be. Gear bag at his feet.

'Ah O'Reilly, you up to get the ride?' The laugh on him then, hacking away, phlegmed up like an auld one on sixty a day, doubled over at the hilarity of himself.

I get right up to him. Go in real close so I can see the flinch of fear tighten at him, grab hold of him around the edges.

'Just so ya know, I'm not making a habit out of this.' The look on him, the reality of what is about to happen dawning on him, his features verging on the arrogant, my grip loosening on him, and I'm not sure that I can give him the satisfaction of this.

'Yeah, Joe, yeah sure,' and he goes to open his bag, on full show, not having to worry or care or contemplate being caught. No Guard ever walking the rhythm of their beat anywhere near this fucking hole of a place. 'So what will it be, bud,' and he's piling all sorts of shit in front of me, pulling it all out in an assortment of baggies.

'Just some charlie will do.'

'Ah here, but that's so boring, unexpected telling the truth, from a man such as yourself and all.'

'I said just coke,' and I'm eying around me now, wanting to make sure I'm not seen, that people won't think I'm in on all this now. For word to be getting out. For word to be getting back to fucking Da.

'Is it for those posh bastards,' and he's nudging me now, like we're friends, like we're fucking associates. 'I'm right, amn't I,' he nudges again, goes rummaging, takes out a tray of benzos. 'They'll love these so. All those pricks with their cheap shiny suits down the quays horse the benzos into them so they do. Nice little earner, these lads.'

'Grand, yeah I'll take that, and the coke,' and he's delighted with himself, taking his time wrapping them up, like he's down the Tesco till packing bags, raising money for the local GAA.

'You're not to tell anyone about this either, yeah, a once-off, for Sabine, her debt is paid, yeah.' He doesn't answer, just continues with his packing; I get myself in a little closer, to make sure that I'm heard, that I'm understood. 'So, stay the fuck away from her, you little prick,' and he's not so delighted with himself now. Starts to square up to me, ready to have his say about the whole thing.

'Fuck you, Joe, you come here thinking you're above all this, that you're better than the rest of us, than your Da, yet here you fucking are.' Now it's time for the smugness. There it is plastered all over his face. I push in closer, put my foot hard on his, shoulder him into the wall, put my face into his, clamp my hand up under his chin, pinning his neck, just like I've seen Da do a thousand fucking times, and I take pleasure in the greyness that comes to his face, in the smugness that vanishes without a trace, in the look of absolute terror that replaces it. I hold on to his neck, the pulse of him thumping right through my arm, the pressure of his scalp against the concrete of the wall, and the energy and life that surges through me with the power and the strength and the smell of it. I push harder.

'You won't say a fucking thing,' I say, spitting each word right into his face.

As I make my way back, I pull out my phone, *I'll bring the gear*, rapid-fired to Johnny, before I have time to change my mind.

/

Sabine insisted that she wanted to come. Wouldn't take no for an answer. Said she was coming whether I wanted her to go or not, and who did I think I was keeping her away from free cocktails. I relented, told her to meet me out front at seven. She's late. No harm, mind you. If we got there too soon we'd look like tools, having to make small talk about the weather, or school, or Jaysus knows. But I didn't want to get there so late either that we couldn't leave early, like I'd planned. I just wanted to drop, and go, but having Sabine there made things just that bit more complicated.

Quarter to eight and she's here, her dusted lilac hair pinned loosely into two Princess Leia-type buns, her familiar skinny blacks and patent Doc boots making their way towards me, in no fucking rush, like.

'Enough glitter, yeah?' I ask, her eyes and lips disco-balling away like ninety.

'Fuck off,' she says, leaning into me, linking her arm through mine.

'What's with the puffer,' she says, nodding at the big lump of a coat on me. Trying to prise it off my shoulders.

'Get to fuck,' I say, nudging her off me, pushing her away.

'Jaysus, all right,' she says and walks on ahead, and I can feel the blister of the gear against my chest, hoping that the bulge of it can't be seen.

We get to Johnny's coming on nine, which is a nice one all round. We would be safe leaving at half ten, excuses of the last train on our lips. As we're walking his street, it's the calmness that unsettles, the peacefulness of it, the detachment of the houses, the sparkle of the four-wheel drives out the front, the background hush of the sea, the maturity of the oaks with their whispering leaves, promising protection, promising opportunities.

Bonnie Mitchell opens the door, all tanned and cashmere.

'Joe,' she says, and quickly pulls me into her, kisses placed either side of my cheeks, her smoked perfumed scent suffocating the air.

'We're all so delighted that you could make it,' she says, and how the lies come so easily to her.

Mrs Mitchell sent a card. In place of her presence at the funeral. To Ma when she heard. It was in an envelope so heavy and paper so thick it needed two stamps. In the time before, I would have reused that paper, I would have imagined how it would soak up my ink, how it would work against the black of my pen. But it just lay in the bin after, not a second glance given.

'They're all in the marquee out back,' she says, leading us in, saying a quick hello to Sabine, welcoming her as 'Joe's dear friend', as our feet sink right into the depth of the cream woollen carpet. 'Keep the mess contained, is what I say, it leaves it easier for tomorrow's clean-up too, and also lets you have a bit of privacy away from the oldies. Am I right,' she says, giving us a wink, and Sabine is at me, her excitement worn all over her, 'Stay friends with Johnny' muttered under her breath.

The marquee is huge and crowded. Dance floor in the middle, a bar at either side, and a DJ pumping tunes I'm too Joe Sixpack to appreciate.

'Bleedin' amazing,' Sabine shouts, pulling at my hand as we make our way through the crowd of endless faces. Some I recognise, most I don't. No one registers me. A blank stare looking through you far worse than a disgusted reaction.

'Come on, let's dance,' Sabine says, pulling my hand towards the dance floor.

'Ah you're all right,' I resist. 'I'm just going to get me a drink first.' She is off before I'm finished, joining the crowd on the dance floor, as if she's been part of this world forever. Not seeing or feeling the divide like I do.

It's then that I notice Johnny, surrounded by the rugby team all reminiscing on last week's victory.

'What's with the big fuck-off coat,' he laughs, not getting the discomfort.

'Inside,' I whisper, not making myself obvious at all.

'Oh, right, yeah,' he says, winking at me, and then breaking into a laugh, as if this is all just some game, no big deal.

Once we're inside, and well out of sight, I take out the stash I have hidden in the lining. I can see Johnny's eyes light up, drinking in all the detail, happy to see how it *goes down* and all I can think of is Jarvis Cocker's 'Common People' in the back of my head, playing itself on fucking repeat.

'Nice one, Joe, fucking nice one,' as he reaches out to take what I've got. He leaves it on the side cabinet and moves into his pocket for his distressed leather wallet, the Louis Vuitton marking so subtle you'd hardly notice it, but unmistakably there all the same. 'I made sure to get cash – you know, no trace,' as if we were on an episode of fucking *Love/Hate*. 'Got you a mark-up too, we're happy to pay for it, you're not putting anyone out, you know that Joe, don't you,' and the absolute obliviousness of him, the money fanning out in front of him.

I grab it, stuff it into my pocket, and fling my puffer into the corner, wanting to get it as far away from me as possible. He's still standing there, arm outstretched, the money that greased his long soft fingers meaning absolutely nothing to him.

'Joe, you do know it would have been OK if you couldn't bring this stuff.' The smile is gone from him now, and he's putting his wallet back into his pocket. 'Seriously, it really wouldn't have mattered,' completely ignorant of how much all this matters to me. 'I never would have asked if I knew it would affect us,' and he puts his hand on my shoulder.

'Ah look, you're all right,' I say, giving his hand a pat, signalling it's OK for him to take his down, 'there's other stuff going on, it's complicated, but just don't ask me to do this again,' and it comes out fiercer than I intend, I see the sharpness of it in the flinch of his face. 'This is the one and only time I'll ever do this, OK?' I continue, really needing him to understand that this can't be what I'm known for.

'Yeah, of course, no problem, and sorry,' he says, and hovers, not sure what to do next.

'All right, I'm off to the bar so,' I say, getting him off the hook, 'are ya coming?'

'Ah you're grand, I'll get this stuff sorted.' He starts packing the gear into a bag, ready to start handing out, like party favours.

'Chat to ya so,' I say, and make my way through.

I get to the bar and I see her before she sees me. Naoise. My heart thumps just that bit harder. Fuck.

I pretend to busy myself with the drinks menu. A fucking drinks menu, a real one. For a house party. I scan to make it look like I haven't seen her, or don't feel her coming closer to me.

'Joe,' she says, putting her arms right around me, kissing me hard, parting my lips with her tongue, and her head is back now laughing, her toppling over herself. 'I'm so fucking drunk, Joe,' she slurs into my ear, all polished and free, and it's more than the drink, I can tell by the buzz of her, by the chew of her cheek.

'Ah howya,' I say, drinks menu still in hand, still trying to catch my breath, still tasting the tang of her, unsure of what to do next, or where to put my hands, or where in her space I should be.

'Have you decided yet?' she asks, breaking through my anxiousness with a tapping at the menu in my hand, sitting herself into my lap. 'I can recommend the pink flamingo,' she says, and I start to laugh, wrap my arms around her waist, and leave them there, fingers sprawled on her thighs, connecting us, making us fit.

'All right so,' I say, game for the challenge.

'Two pink flamingos when you're ready,' I say to the barman, who looks pissed off to fuck being giving orders by jumped-up little tossers, his face brightening slightly at my accent.

She can't stay still, she's up looking around, then back down, and 'This fucking song,' she screams, pulling at me to get up, dancing in the gap between us, pulling at my arms.

'Two pink flamingos, sir,' the barman says, placing two sparkling concoctions in front of us, complete with flashing pink ice cube and pink-flamingoed umbrella. She takes hers, places the umbrella behind her ear, and downs it in one. Takes mine then and does the same.

'This fucking song,' she says again, spinning herself out of my reach. And then I see him, Phonsie Dunphy, in a ring with the lads on the dance floor, breaking away, shouting towards us.

'Naoise, over here,' he says, him all buzz too, and she's leaving, moving towards him, he picks her up, her squealing, and they go into the centre of the jumping ring, all concealed and uniformed with belonging, and I just stay, not calling out, not trying to join in.

I'm getting myself up off the stool, and the heaviness of it, trying to scan for Sabine. I battle my way through the dance floor, through arm-joined barriers jumping in time to 'Maniac', searching for Sabine, wading through the dancers, and stumblers, and moshers, all bumper to bumper, looking for her, wanting to firmly plant my suggestion of leaving. But no sign. Typical. I try my phone, no answer. I get to the house and enter the long-carpeted hallway, go to try the phone again when I see Naoise, and Phonsie Dunphy, at the door by the study. Him all over her. Pulling and dragging at her, his lips on hers. Roughly. She is not responding; she is practically unconscious, limply trying to resist.

'Get the fuck off her,' I say, pulling Dunphy back, taking him by surprise.

'Fuck off, O'Reilly,' he says. 'This is none of your business, but I'll be finished in about half an hour if you want a go of her then.' He turns his back to me, trying to get Naoise through the door of the study, trying to slam me out. And my heart starts to race, really fucking pump, my hands sweating, my tongue not swallowing, and all this saliva is gathered and swirling around in my mouth, with nowhere at all to fucking go.

'Get away from her now, Phonsie, or I swear to fuck I'm busting your fucking face.'

He lets out an entitled laugh, 'Well, my baby's got the Benz, thanks to you,' and I punch him, hard, in the side of his ribs, winding him, giving me enough time to get her, but I feel the shake in my hands, my knees, the thump of my chest ringing hard in my ears. I did this, I brought this shit here. I bring her towards the bathroom, splash water on her face, trying to get her to stay with me, I lean her over the bath and stick my fingers down her throat, until she gags, until she retches up the pills she's taken, I do it again, to make sure, she's sobbing now, shivering, I place her head on my lap, my jumper over her shoulders and take out my phone and ring Johnny.

'I'm in your bathroom, yeah the downstairs one, come quick, it's Naoise, and phone an ambulance.' I stroke her hair as she sobs, chat to her gently, tell her it will be OK and I'm rubbing my hands on my jeans now, trying to calm my breathing, calm myself down, trying not to let the guilt eat right into the nerves of me, I can feel it seeping, soaking me right through. The door slams open, Mr and Mrs Mitchell rushing to their daughter, a superior fuck of a smile on Phonsie Dunphy hovering behind them.

'What did she take,' I yell at Phonsie, ignoring the looks of shock, the mutterings of denials from the parents. Mrs Mitchell has now started to cry, sobbing right there along with her daughter, she has taken over from me, has her now cradled to herself, lullaby rocking, back and forth.

'She's gotten most of it up,' I reassure her, 'but we'll need to know what she took for the paramedics, when they get here,' and she turns to Phonsie now too, pleading with him to let her know. Her voice erratic, escalating with each plea.

'Ask Joe, he's the one who brought it,' he says, not an etch of a lie visible anywhere near him and the shame of it is all me, heavier than I ever thought possible.

'Bonnie, I'm calling the Guards,' Johnny's Da calls out, but I don't register yet that this is not going well for me, not until I realise that they are all looking at me. Until I realise what that look on their faces means, and sure isn't it true what they say, like father like son, that tarred brush a magnet, only attracted to scum like me.

Finn

'Back again, Mrs O'Reilly? What seems to be the problem this time?' Dr Flynn asked, barely looking up from his computer screen. I wondered what he had on it. *Minecraft*, *Candy Crush*, or the last level of *Plants vs. Zombies*? I didn't think I'd look up from that either, especially if I hadn't passed a checkpoint yet.

'Show him, Finn,' Ma said, pulling at my arms, making me stretch them out, right in front of him.

He sat up now, straight in his chair. Took my arms and looked them over and over.

'Can you take your jumper off for me, Finn, good lad.' He was inspecting my arms closely. I could see the hair up his nose, black and springy, like John Joe McGinty's labradoodle.

'Has he any more?' he asked Ma.

'Yes, Doctor, all up the backs of his legs as well.' He inspected those too. Ma was sat still. Ma was never still. She was always drumming, or tapping, or chewing on that hard skin around her nails, until it bled.

'How did he get them?' Dr Flynn asked, still inspecting.

'Chasing, Doctor. He swears it. And swinging off the bicycle rack in school. That's what—'

'How quickly did they appear?' he asked.

'Straight away, and they're getting worse, darker.'

Dr Flynn was writing on his computer. His fingers flying like the feckin' Flash. I didn't think anyone could type that fast. Now Rebecca Burke could have given him a run for his money; she helped her Da out at the shop at the weekend, sometimes even on a school day, when she'd come in late with her lips and tongue blue from sucking on blueberry bonbons. But Dr Flynn was like a champion of speed typing, if there ever was such a thing.

'I'm contacting a friend of mine. A specialist. Immediately,' he said. 'She'll see him quickly, on my recommendation.'

'Jesus, Doctor. What do you think it is?'

'I can't be sure, Mrs O'Reilly. He needs further testing, blood work, but this along with the nosebleeds could mean something else.'

'What else?' Ma asked, leaning forward with her two hands gripped on to the side of her chair. Her knuckles white, I couldn't see her fingers, tucked under tight. The scab of her fag burn was starting to crack. It was a mistake. Da usually put them places where nobody would see.

'I really can't say, but we need to get it investigated, and the quicker the better.'

Ma hadn't moved.

'Have you thought about getting a medical card, Mrs O'Reilly? I'm sure you'd qualify.'

'No, Doctor, it's not for us. Frank doesn't like us sponging off the state.'

'Why don't you just fill in the form. I can get Sheila to go through it with you, in the back room?'

'He checks the post.'

'Fill in the form anyway, Mrs O'Reilly. We can see about the rest of it later.' He placed his hand on Ma's arm. Gently.

'You can pop on your jumper again there, Finn, there's a good man. Would you like a lollipop, or are you too old for that now?'

'No, Doctor, a lollipop would be great.' I rummaged right down to the bottom of the container to get a green one. Everyone knows that lime is the best. I wondered what the specialist was, or did. A specialist of bruises? Of nose-bleeds? Well, as long as I got a day off school, they could specialise away.

Joe

They arrive at the house, quicker than necessary, no flash of blue here to distress the neighbours. They know who to go for too, the Guards who arrive, don't even have to ask as if 'scumbag' was tattooed right on my forehead.

'What's going on,' and it's Johnny at the door, with Sabine, holding hands, although dropped as soon as they enter.

'This hooligan of yours has only gone and drugged your sister, that's what,' says Mr Mitchell, making a show of pacing the room, clinking the cubes of his double distilled cognac. The Guard closest to me takes out his cuffs and with a 'Hands behind your back' clicks them tight into place and begins walking me out of the room.

'Is this really necessary?' Johnny asks, and the question is aimed right at his Da. 'Seriously, Dad, it's not Joe's fault, I asked him,' but his father has turned his back, making his way towards his wife and daughter, crouching down beside them on the white marbled tiles.

'Can I come too,' Sabine says, now moving closer to where I am, trying to feed her strength directly to me as I'm hustled right out of the door. 'I want to come too,' she asks again, but is met with a stare that signals a no. 'Which station so,' she asks rushing after us, determined to get what she wants.

'Pearce Street, love,' one of them answers, obviously new to the job, obviously pissing off her partner who now has one more thing to add to the list of what-not-to-dos around skangers like me. We're not fucking worthy, you see.

'Thanks for not resisting,' the young one says, while dipping my head into the back of the car, and earns herself another glare from her partner. 'What', she mouths as the other shakes his head and turns up his radio to put a stop to any notions of conversation.

The new ones are always clueless. Watching too much crime TV, expecting a fight on arrest. Preconceived notions of what we with our accents, our out-of-place faces, our disadvantaged postcodes, will do to resist you. But we won't open our mouths. We'll go quietly and silently. We won't resist or assist or do anything that will make them take it the fuck out on us. No comment to the no comments. Always.

We pull up to the station and up to the hatch, flicked open to see what fresh meat is now got.

'Name and address, son,' says a balding head, too bored to look up, to take notice of me or what I have done.

'Joe O'Reilly,' I say. 'Liberty Mansions,' I add; I get a proper look then.

'O'Reilly?' A really good look. A second look, not so fucking bored now like. 'Frank's lad?' The penny has dropped; the two either side of me tighten their grip. 'Hey, Skinner,' he shouts, right into the back. 'Out here, we've Frank O'Reilly's lad,' and Skinner's out to get a good look too.

'Welcome.' Skinner comes round, wants to do the honours of taking me in. 'We had bets on, you know,' he says, opening the doors with his lanyard and pin, and smooth clean white hands, while leading me back into the holding cells. 'Wondering when you'd make your appearance.'

It takes all of my might not to tell him to fuck right off.

'Frank's fucking lad,' he says, shaking his head, locking me in tight, whistling some unrecognisable shite all the way back to his room. All fucking delighted with himself.

Finn

Jasmine's Ma was at the counter, piling Nutella toast high onto the plate beside her. Me and Dunner nicked a slice before she had a chance to get it to the table; you'd never get a slice then.

'Oi, keep your hands off, ya little shits,' she said, shielding the rest with her arm and elbow. Nudging us away.

Jasmine's flat was always fruit de loop. She had two sisters and two brothers, the horrible twins, all of them younger than her. Ma said she needed a double dose of Nurofen when visiting or else her head would be busted for days.

'Newsflash. We're not allowed nuts in school,' Jasmine said, mouth full, fresh teeth-marks indicating her territory on the slice in her hand.

'Fuck sake, Jasmine, just eat the toast, you're not in school yet,' her Ma said while flinging lunchboxes into open school bags by the front door.

'I'll have nut germs all over me fingers,' she said, wiggling hers in front of the twins, trying to make them laugh.

'Go and bleedin' wash them, so. I'm warning ya, don't go hyping the bejaysus out of them before you're about to leg it. I'm hoping for a quiet morning, thank you very much.'

'Right so,' Jasmine said, picking up her school bag and

giving her Ma a hug. 'But if someone collapses and dies because of my Nutella breath, it's on you,' she said, breathing hard on her Ma's face as she headed for the door.

'Get away with you, ya wagon,' her Ma laughed after her, whipping the back of her school bag with a wet tea towel, the Christmas pudding one, the one that is always slung across her shoulder.

'And wait for your sisters,' she called as Jasmine pulled the door closed.

We waited for Frida and Layla, like always, by the rail of the stairs. Always the stairs, not the lift. There were no bannisters in the lift, nothing to get a good slide down.

'Keep your distance, you know the drill,' she warned as her spits came running towards us, red curls bobbing just like Jasmine's. But you wouldn't tell her that, she'd give you a shit-kicking if you even dared. 'And no earwigging either, do you hear me, or I'll tell Da it was youse who burnt the sitting-room curtains last week,' she said, her arms folded like her Ma's mini-me.

I mimicked her cross face, hand on hip, wagging finger, behind her back. Their giggling faces gave me away; Jasmine shot me a look.

'Did nothing, swear it,' I said, crossing my heart with my fingers.

We let Frida and Layla walk on ahead. 'That way we can keep an eye,' Jasmine said as she placed herself in the middle of me and Dunner, linking arms. 'Now spill, what did the doctor say? Does he think it's your Da like Mrs O'Sullivan?

Was he still wearing his Ma's jeans?' She fired question after question.

'He hasn't a clue. He said he needs to send me to a specialist,' I said.

'What type of bleedin' doctor doesn't even know what's wrong with you?'

'And what even is a specialist anyways?' Dunner asked.

'Don't have a budgie's, but Ma said it's on Wednesday, so no homework, no school, no David Mannion's eggy sandwiches.'

'Every day with those sandwiches, what's that all about?' said Dunner, and I'm already gagging just thinking about it.

'I'm going to be a specialist when I grow up,' Jasmine said.

'Specialist me arse, sure you don't even know what it is,' Dunner said, booting the stone in front of him, hard.

'Ah go and shite,' Jasmine said, giving him a dead arm. 'Da says I can be whatever I want to be when I grow up.'

'Where does he think you're from, the bleedin' Fox of the Rock? Ah look, there's Shane,' he said, waving in his direction. 'Hey Shane. Shane, wait up.' And he's gone, running.

'I will be a specialist, you know, if I want to,' Jasmine said, and she had that face on her, the exact same one like when Mr Fahy said she needn't bother joining the school quiz team. Her arms folded and her eyes nearly black.

'Since when have you ever listened to Dunner? Sure he thinks there are leprechauns at Dublin Zoo,' I said, and we laugh.

'Do you promise to tell me what they do? The specialist, that is? You know, see if it's worth my while?'

'Sure, missus,' I said. 'Now race ya to the gate.'

'Hey, not fair, you got a head start.'

But I'm not listening – I'm nearly there, and for once I'm winning.

Joe

The holding cell is smoke-filled and stale, not much different to pretty much anywhere else on a Friday night. A drunken rendition of 'Streets of New York' has taken hold, three fucking months too early, making no difference as most of them start joining in. I take to a spot right in the corner, and back myself in with my head right on down. I'm used to keeping myself invisible, I know how to keep myself well out of the mix.

I start to think about Naoise, hope to fuck that she doesn't think that I would do something like that to her. As if I would ever do something like that to her. I think back to our last moments, how I got her the drink. But the barman gave it straight to us, handed it straight to her, and I know that she wouldn't think that of me. Well, I think I fucking know. But there, hammering away at the back of my skull, is what I know to be true: I was the one who provided the gear, who allowed that to happen to her.

They say there is no harm in it, that it's nothing to do with them if someone ODs, gets shot, done for possession, whatever. I've heard those excuses roll off Da's tongue as sleep-deprived mothers with their bags of anxiety begged and pleaded with him to get their young ones out of that world. The dealing. The using. Always and forever met with a *nothing to do with me, love* or a *fuck right off.*

'Ya haven't a light, have ya,' I'm asked, by a sidler that I know by the head on him is looking for the chats.

'Sorry, bud,' and I turn my focus back into myself, so he'll get the fucking hint, like.

'What'd they bring ya in for?' He's breathing right down my neck; I can almost taste his Abrakebabra fries and cocktail of lagers, injecting my nose with his smells.

'Look, I'm just minding me business, yeah,' and I pull myself further away, tucking myself closer to that corner I'm in. Getting his stink and his leer off of me.

'So it's like that, ya prick, just trying to pass the time, so I am. Little fucking prick,' but he's already starting to move away and goes to annoy the fuck out of someone else, but not many in form for that shite. Right.

'Streets of New York' is now on round three, my head is pounding, my thoughts of what happened are having time to fester, grow dark, spread out, take root, and I don't feel like snapping out of it, or any of those things that I usually do.

'O'Reilly,' a Guard calls – how long have I been there, three hours, four? 'You're out, come on,' he calls again, the impatience rising in his thick on-the-job voice, already fed up with his lot.

Back up to the hatch to collect my possessions, wallet and phone, and the gobshite from the back comes out for one last gawk.

'You got lucky, O'Reilly?' he says, mouth full of a meatball sub. 'Not pressing charges they say,' in between chews.

There is a dollop of sauce staining his chin, making him look like a tit. 'But it won't be long till you're back. You can be sure of that, just like your Da,' and he's back into his box.

I hear a scrape of a chair as I move towards the entrance – Sabine. Her hair now loose, her eyeliner smudged all down her face, and she wraps her arms tight around me into a hug.

'She doesn't think I spiked her, does she?' I look into her eyes; I can tell if she's trying to hide anything, Sabine can't lie for shit, so she can't. She just stays there, holding either side of my arms, holding my eyes with hers, but not saying anything at all. 'You think I did,' I say, trying to shake her off, trying to get her away from me, but she holds firm.

'No, Joe,' she says, but her look is still firm, her hands still clasped at my elbows, steadying me, 'I don't think you did it,' and it's then that she looks down, that she gives herself away. 'I know you brought it,' she says, and it's barely a whisper. 'I was with Johnny, when he was passing it around, them all toasting you in your absence, delighted with themselves.'

I can physically feel the hurt in her voice.

'Please say that it wasn't for me.' She's looking hard at me now. 'Joe, please,' and I hug her tight, she hugs me tight back, but I can't shake off the grime, the drilling thought of know-ing, that absolutely everyone was right about me all along.

Finn

The specialist didn't look too special to me. She didn't even have a cool coat or T-shirt or anything. How were you supposed to know that she even *was* the specialist?

'Hi, Finn. My name is Caroline,' she said when we were sitting down. She had pictures of butterflies and fairies and pirates on her walls. I wanted to tell her that they were babyish. That she needed to get ones for older kids like me, but to be fair they didn't look too bad, and the pirates were funny enough, I supposed, if you were into that type of thing. I'd say it next time, if there was one, or let Dr Flynn know, maybe he'd pass on the message for me. Do her a favour, you know, she could be embarrassing older kids with that type of thing. But not me, yet, I thought. But you'd never know when that could change.

'I am a haematologist,' she said, and I started to giggle a little and looked at Ma. She hadn't the foggiest either.

'That means that I know everything there is to know about blood,' she said.

'Like Dracula?' I asked.

'Yes, just like Dracula,' she said, 'but I use needles instead of fangs.' She laughed, showing off a mouth full of metal braces. Braces. On an adult. Sure what would an adult need with straight teeth?

'Dr Flynn sent you to me, because he was a little worried about your bruises and nosebleeds. I'm just going to do a few little tests this morning to see if we can figure out what's causing all this. OK?'

'OK,' I replied.

'I'll be using two different needles. This one here,' she lifted one off the table, 'will be used in your arm, to take some blood samples, probably about three, so we can get a really good look at it.'

'Do you have to put that in three times?' I asked, not so sure I was OK with these tests any more. I decided I preferred Mrs O'Sullivan's Friday tests, and that was really saying something, because I was really useless at them, even when I studied and all. Joe said sometimes it just took my brain a little bit longer for things to stick. But at least I knew what to expect with those.

'No, pet, we just need to put it in once, and then we attach these little vials, and once one is full we swap it. I promise I'll be super quick,' Caroline said. The specialist.

'But what about that big needle there. Are you going to be using that one too?' I figured I didn't need these tests after all. There was no need, sure Shane didn't get any of this done when he broke his leg that time, and that was much worse than bruises, everyone knew that.

'Yes, Finn, this is the second test I have to do. It's called a bone marrow test. I have to put this needle into your hip, and then take out a sample of your bone marrow, that's the spongy stuff on the inside of your bones.' And all I kept thinking of was those Markies treats that Jasmine's dog Rex loves, the ones with the marrowbone and gravy. Was that the same stuff as bone marrow? Could you eat mine with gravy?

'Will we start?' she asked, and before I could answer she had my arm out.

'Now I'm going to rub a little cream on your arm here,' she said, tickling the inside of my arm with her finger, 'just to numb the area a little, and then a quick little injection in your hip before I take the sample, again just to numb the pain. I promise I'll be as quick as I can. Mum, maybe if you sit on my far side. Finn, you just keep your eyes on Mum, OK?'

Ma was over in a flash, gripped my hand in hers, locked her eyes onto mine.

'It'll be all right, love, over in a minute, just keep looking at me, love,' she said, but her grip was tightening and starting to hurt.

I barely felt the one in my arm, and I counted the vials as they were lined up on the desk, one, two, three. The one in the hip really, really hurt though, even more than that time I got my fingers slammed in the front door. A big sharp pain, like someone jabbed my bone with a knife and wiggled and waggled it around. Hard. But Caroline was right, she was quick, and it was finished before I had a chance to really cry.

'All done, pet,' Caroline said, pressing some cotton wool onto my hip and placing a plaster over it. 'I've pulled a few strings,' she said to Ma, 'cleared some space for a slot in the lab, so the results should be back this evening, if you're able to wait and come back?'

'We'll come back,' Ma said.

'Great job, Finn. Would you like a pirate sticker?' said Caroline.

'Ah no, you're grand,' I said. I really had to get on to Dr Flynn about that; imagine her thinking I'd be into pirates, I'm bleedin' twelve.

Ma took me to the cinema while we waited. *Avengers: Infinity War*, with the whole lot of them, Iron Man, Spi-der-Man, Black Panther, all on one screen. The Guardians of the Galaxy even made the cut.

We got a big popcorn too, and a Coke. Each. And sour jel-lies. Not even from the shop like, but from the cinema kiosk. Ma never did that. We always brought our own. But not today. We even had time for a McDonald's after, and she let me get a Big Mac instead of the usual Happy Meal, which confirmed everything right up for me there, so it did. Ma had officially gone mad. She kept staring at me, when she thought I couldn't see, and googling on her phone, pulling it close to her chest when I tried to get a good look.

We got back to the hospital about eight o'clock, just like what Caroline told us to, and she was waiting for us, there at the reception, bringing us straight to her office.

'Finn, would you mind waiting out here for a minute, pet, I just want to have a quick word with Mum first,' Caroline said, before Ma or me even had a chance to say anything, before I even got a chance to tell her what film we saw, and how brilliant it was, and how definite I was that she should have a few Avengers stickers to add to her wall collection. And why did she want only Ma? And why wouldn't she let me come in? Why did Ma go without telling me all was OK?

Maybe she thinks it was Da, just like Mrs O'Sullivan. Had she rung the social, told them? Would they take me away like Sasha Quinn and put me in a home, away from Joe? I wanted to go up to the door, put my ear to it, try to hear what they said. But I couldn't. It was too busy and that was too sly, even for me.

The door opened a crack and Ma stuck her head out, her eyes red-rimmed and wet.

'You can come in now, love,' she said, but I couldn't move. I didn't want to hear what they had to say any more.

'It's all right, love, Caroline has something that she needs to tell you,' and she reached out for me, put her arm across my shoulder, squeezed me in tight to her and her smells of lemon and smoke and popcorn. She led me to the chair, the same one as earlier, and left her arm right where it was, all wrapped around me.

'Thank you for waiting, Finn,' Caroline said. 'We got your results back, and I'm afraid it's not great news.' Ma's breath shuddered, all caught in her throat, and her hug tightened, pressing me in too much.

'You have a form of cancer, Finn. It's called acute myeloid leukaemia, but you can call it AML for short, if it's easier,'

95

she said. I looked at Ma, but she looked straight ahead. Nothing about this sounded easy.

'AML is a cancer of the blood, Finn – that is why you were getting those nosebleeds and those nasty bruises. It was your body trying to tell you that your blood was not quite working in the way that it should.' Now I'm wondering if I messed up my blood that time me and Jasmine did blood brothers. Cutting our palms with Joe's penknife and squishing them together. Mixing our blood together forever. What if Jasmine's blood is broken now too like mine?

'How did this happen?' Ma suddenly asked, all whispered and crackled, and I'm afraid to tell her what I think. That this is all because of me. Jasmine didn't even want to do it. I made her because I'd seen it on some show, and I can't even remember its name, and I'd no clue at the time that it meant all this would happen to me.

'No one knows the cause as yet, Mrs O'Reilly. It is a very complicated form of cancer, it is not black and white. We will need to run some more tests, just to determine the best course of treatment, but most definitely we will be starting chemotherapy as soon as possible.'

'Will it hurt?' I asked, positive I couldn't take another big needle in the hip.

'No, pet, it won't. We just need to do a scan, which is like a big X-ray, and a few more blood tests, and that will be all for the moment.'

'What about surgery, can you not just cut it out of him, get it out. Does that not have to happen first?' Ma asked.

'I'm sorry, Mrs O'Reilly, I know this is so difficult to come to terms with, but because leukaemia is a cancer of the blood, that means there is nothing to take out as such. Again, once we do more tests, we will be able to discuss with you in detail Finn's treatment plan.' I didn't want a treatment plan. I just wanted to go home. I needed to get ready for swimming with Joe. We were practising for months, every Saturday, to help me get into Stingrays. We were starting swimming again at school on Monday and there was no way I was using those skanky orange armbands or baby-chewed floats again this year. It was someone else's turn for that slagging. Joe had made sure of it.

'Can we go home now, Ma,' and she couldn't look at me. 'I really just want to go home,' I said again. She still wouldn't look at me.

'I'm so sorry, Finn, but you can't go home just yet, and I am sorry I can't tell you exactly when at the moment. But we will know more once we decide on your treatment plan, and we'll let you know then. I promise.' But her promise wasn't good enough. I didn't want to miss swimming. I didn't want to miss school. I didn't want any of this.

Ma got up then, paced the room, kept her back to me, but I knew by the shake in her shoulders that she was crying. Caroline took out a packet of tissues from her desk, went over to Ma and handed her one.

'What's the success rate, Doctor?' she asked, whispered to her, in case I'd hear.

'Once we get the treatment plan together, Mrs O'Reilly,

Finn's team will sit down with you and go through everything. Today is a shock, I know that. But please make sure to bring your questions. Both of you. As many as you want.'

Ma's shoulders continued to shake, Caroline still at her side, and I just sat there, too afraid to move, to give her a hug, or kiss her cheek, in case I gave her the cancer too.

Joe

I put the key in the latch, and heave my shoulder against the weight of the door, the heat swelling it, making it impossible to sneak the announcement of my arrival. I needn't have worried; Ma is already up, and dressed, and leaning against the counter eating toast.

'Good party so, yeah,' she says, giving a knowing smile.

'Ah all right, Ma,' I say, reaching behind her to put the kettle on.

'It's good to see ya starting to enjoy yourself again, love,' and she puts her hand on my back.

'Do you want one?' I say, taking a mug down from the press, the faded Crunchie one that Da always used.

'Ah no, love, you're grand, had a coffee earlier.' She is looking grand too, the best I've seen her in a while in fairness, and it's nice to see even a sliver of Ma creeping back through the cracks again. Taking my mind off my own.

'I'm going back into work later,' she says, 'just part-time, told Pat I'd only do the day shift mind, till I'm back on me feet right like.' She caresses her left elbow with the palm of her right, her free hand scratching at her neck.

'That's great, Ma, really great,' I look properly at her now, 'but I would've loved to have seen the face on Pat and you telling him that.'

She starts laughing then. 'Ah sure Pat's all mouth, told me it would be full-time or nothing, I told him I'll start back to three days a week, and I'd see him tomorrow.'

Then I start laughing too. 'Sure you'll be back to running the place in no time, Ma.'

'More like putting manners on the lot of them, love.' She ruffles the top of my head, like she used to, like she used to do to Finn, and I turn to pour the water into my mug, watch as the teabag brews.

'I was in to see your Da yesterday—'

'Ma. Don't.'

'He misses you, Joe.' I bring my tea to the couch, not wanting this chat again, not wanting to fight with Ma, not today, when she is finally pulling the pieces back together.

'He asked me to give you this.' She takes an envelope from the top drawer, the one where she keeps the swarming bills, all jammed in, hardly able to keep it shut.

'He wants to see you, Joe, wants you to come in to visit.' She lays the envelope on the arm of the couch, places her palm lightly on my forearm, takes it away just as quick, leaving the breath of her imprint on me.

'I'll see ya later, OK,' she says as she's putting on her jacket, grabbing her bag from the table, leaning over to give the top of my head a kiss.

'Read it, love,' and she's out the door. She can easily forgive and forget, think that it's OK that he abandoned us to all this.

I pick up the envelope; it's the same as all the others,

thinking that the discreet black print in the upper left-hand corner makes the property of Mountjoy Prison any less obvious. It's been opened too. Like all the rest. Sellotaped seal stamped, to show it was read and deemed appropriate for mailing. My hand hovers over the seal. I could phone the Governor if I wanted. Tell him I didn't want to receive any letter. I saw that in the booklet Ma got, on prisoners' rights, the first time Da went in.

I turn it back over, bring it right to the bin, am about to drop it, just like the others with its Sellotaped reseal left intact, but I don't. I fold it over, and zip it into my jacket pocket. Tight.

Finn

Cancer. They said I had cancer. Do kids even get cancer? I thought it was just for auld ones like Shane's Granda or Rebecca's Ma.

Shane's Granda died. From the cancer. But Ma said it was from all the smoking and he was really old and stuff. Rebecca's Ma, well, she just went bald. I saw it when she was picking up Rebecca from school once, and I pointed and pulled at Ma, asking why she'd no hair left. She shushed me and whispered, 'Because of the cancer, God love her.'

I didn't mind going bald. Da was nearly bald. He kept his head shaved tight, so it looked bald, but with little small spikes, warning you away. I liked rubbing my hand on his head and feeling the bristles of those spikes tickling my hand. He'd let me do it sometimes, usually when it was freshly shaved. 'Feel here, Finney boy,' he'd say, rubbing my hand over the top. But other times he'd tell me to get away the fuck, slapping my hand off him.

I still wasn't allowed to go home. Even though I'd had all their tests. I may need more, so the doctor said. I hoped they'd let Ma bring in my pyjamas soon; I was in this weird apron thing with teddies on it and I wasn't allowed to wear my jocks, so my bum was on show all the time, which was really scarlet for me. The nurses and the doctors seen it so they did, my bum, when I had to jump on the bed to get into that big coffin of a yoke. I had to lie down flat and stay really still and then they pushed a button that slowly brought me into it, with lights like a spaceship or a time machine, they said. But it really wasn't like that at all. I couldn't breathe properly, I couldn't see, I was trapped right in. It was worse than the needle taking that spongy stuff from my hip. But I kept still. Nurse Sarah, with the big smiley face and the strawberry-smelling hair, said I'd have to just do it again if I didn't keep still. So I did, and started to count sheep in my head to try to distract me, just like she told me to do. 'A little trick,' she said. But they were just too hard to count. They kept running away, not wanting to jump the fence I made for them.

I was in a room now on my own. I had a TV too, with the remote all to myself. It was painted in lots of different colours, the room was, all blues and greens and pinks, and it looked just like Dollymount Strand. It even had octopuses and mermaids and fish and sharks, peeking out between the waves, saying hello. Da would say it was like a baby's fucking room. I didn't mind it too much.

I heard Ma on the phone to Da earlier, just outside my room. She was crying and I could hear the muffled shouts from the other side. It sounded like Da was crying too. I've never seen Da cry. He tells us that crying is a sign of weakness. That boys don't cry. That boys should never cry. So we don't. Ever. Unless we're in private, when nobody sees.

Da was here now; Ma had just gone down to get him, to show him where to go. To show him how to find my room. I hoped they'd let him stay. I hoped he'd tell me that they're wrong, that they made a mistake, that I don't have the cancer after all.

Nurse Sarah said I was lucky to get the room on my own. 'Usually you're all packed in like sardines,' she said. I didn't feel so lucky. I had no one to play with, no one to talk to, and no one to ask if getting the cancer meant that you die.

Ma said kids don't die of cancer, but the specialist never said anything. She didn't agree with Ma, she just said nothing, and looked away, so I wasn't really so sure of that now.

Joe

I can see that my locker is open before I reach it, door swinging on its hinges, indicating a lock freshly picked. I'm bracing myself for another hunt for my books, pricking my ears for their routine guffaws, waiting for the inevitable fucking show-time of making the povo search for his stuff, played on repeat for when the natives get bored.

I hate having to give a shit about what's in my locker, that my stuff is not so easily replaced, that my stuff is forever connected to the veins of broken skin cracking Ma's hands, and the deep dark set of the bags under her eyes, from the months and months of overtime she gave, for those books, for that stuff, a second thought always having to be given.

I reach the locker and put my hand in, scan carefully, everything still there, thank fuck, but the relief I feel is boiling the anger in me more than it should, seething right to the brim of me, and it's then that I see it. Painted bright red. *Scum.* All neat and cursive, not done in any rush like, right at the back filling the full of my vision. I take a sharp look around, to see who's on hand to make sure that I'll know my place. But no one's about. The senior corridor empty, and graffitiing lockers is not something that St Augustine boys would ever dream to waste their time on, I'd be reminded, but here I am, staring at their handiwork.

First class maths and I make it to my seat, to an accompaniment of snide whispers, 'skanger', 'druggie', 'dealer'. Johnny keeps trying to catch my eye, but my head is down, hoping he'll look away, leave me alone. He tries to get to me after class, Johnny that is, trying to get my attention.

'Hey,' he says, right at my shoulder.

'Johnny, please mate, just leave it, yeah,' and it's the mate that catches, that throws me off guard, how much his friendship meant to me, how much I actually needed him here.

'Look, Joe, I'm sorry,' he says, finally stopping me, getting me to look at him. 'Seriously, I can't tell you how sorry I am, I should never have—'

'I can't do this,' I say, but he keeps pushing at me, even as I'm walking away, trying to step in time with me.

'Naoise is doing great too, well, back to bossing us about the place, and asking for you, a lot, so the usual.' He laughs, I continue to ignore. 'Silver lining, no charges were pressed,' he says, completely failing to make light of the situation. 'I told Dad, I told him if he did, I would tell the Guards it was all me.' The breath in me pushes harder against the rigid top-buttoned noose of my collar, choking, tightening with each gasp taken.

'So, I should be grateful?' The force of me stops him, but he still doesn't understand. My fingers make their way under my collar, pinching at my neck, feeling the sharp burn of it, over and over. He has nothing else to say and I leave him there, open mouth gaping.

I spot Mr Broderick on up ahead, and I duck down the next corridor, not wanting to answer questions about how I'm getting on, or whether I have talked to Ms Smith about my catch-up classes yet. But he's seen me.

'Joe,' he calls after me, the exit is straight ahead, 'Joe,' he calls again, louder this time, firmer, but I'm nearly there, 'Joe,' he says, right at my heel now, but I push on the bar of the door, he puts his hand over it to block.

'What is it, what's going on?' he says. I keep my eyes fixed on the bar, on the exit. 'If you leave, I have no choice but to issue another slip, that's a suspension.' I keep my focus, keep my hand on the bar.

'Come back to the office, even if you want a bit of time to yourself, just come back in.' He takes his hand down, leaving my path clear and I push myself out, don't look back, run, until I get to the bus shelter, sit on the familiar cigarette-burned luminous orange seat. It's there as I'm sitting that I feel it jagging into my side. Zipped in tight in my inside pocket. Da's letter. I take it out, and without a second thought, rip it open, and start to read.

Finn

Da came in on his own, a stuffed plastic chippy bag swinging at his wrist, rain dripping off his nose and black leather jacket. That jacket was Da. It was in photos all over the flat, him and Ma, when they were younger than Joe, on the back of a bus, and Da in that jacket still.

'Your Ma's out havin' a smoke,' he said and sat down at the side of the bed, put his big arms around me and pulled me into his hug. I could hear his heart thump, all strong in his chest, while the drops from his jacket soaked right to my skin, and I just hugged him closer to me.

'You doing all right, bud, yeah?' he asked, breaking away, rubbing my hair, straight back to doing what Da usually did, and as quickly as that it's as if the hug never happened at all.

'I wasn't sure, son, what ya needed like,' he said, dumping the bag's contents all over the bed, 'but your Ma said to make sure there was pyjamas, whatever about anything else,' and he shot me a wink, and the two of us laughed and I took a good look at what else he had brought. Fizzy colas, Taytos and a big bottle of Lucozade, not bad like, but Ma would have remembered that I don't like Lucozade, and she would have remembered that I prefer salt and vinegar, and she definitely would have brought my DS and games. But then I saw it, still trapped in the bag, my favourite

Transformer, and sure Ma would never have thought of that. I reached on down and pulled him right out and remembered the time when I got him. That day at the fun-fair, with Da, Ma and Joe, and the lights of the rides and the big lumps of candyfloss, spinning on waltzers till we were all nearly sick, and then Da winning my Transformer in a big game of hoops that he was able to crack even though it was rigged.

'Ah look, you've a telly an' everything, Finney, go on, budge over there, son,' and he hopped up on the bed, with his shoes on and all, not even caring about the mud mank-ing up the sheets. He gave the channels a good flick through, and settled on the RTÉ News, and not even the news, the thing that's on before it, with those long bell yokes where everyone is supposed to pray.

'Here, Da, look at this,' I said, trying to fill the boredom, and pushed the bed button that made it go up. Da didn't look too impressed, and I started to wish I had just watched the news, and now I thought he was going to bust one, and why did I need to butt in.

'Ah sure go on now, give us a shot of that,' he said, and he grabbed the remote straight out of my hand, smiled at me and showed off his front cracked tooth, while pushing the buttons up and down to ninety.

'Hey, Frank, you can't be doing that, you'll only go and break it,' Ma said, coming in through the door.

'Ah break it me hole, come on, love, get up.' But she just stood there looking, arms folded and cross.

'Come on, Annie,' he said, patting the place beside him. I thought for a minute she'd just make us stop, that she'd get us back to watching the news, but instead she looked at the door, then hopped on up too.

'Nice one, Annie,' Da said, and he squeezed her hand, and kissed her cheek, and the three of us huddled right in, breaking the crap out of the bed. No funfair like, but it would do all the same.

Joe

I give a loud knock, sharp with the knuckles this time.

'Ah Joe, you coming in,' the door opened wide. I ignore and rummage into my bag, take out the envelope and hand it to him.

'There's eight hundred there,' I say as he goes to open it, 'six hundred for Sabine, the extra yo-yos for yourself to keep your mouth shut.' I zip up my bag, flinging it back onto my right shoulder. 'Not a fucking word to Dessie, yeah, Gertie came and paid it off,' I say, holding his gaze, 'that's the story, yeah.'

I stay, waiting for him to confirm it.

'Yes?' I say again, more forcefully this time, in between his muttered counting.

'All right, all right, yes, Gertie brought it, Scout's honour,' and he's holding up his fingers, giving the *surf's up* salute.

I get to the stairwell and on up to Sabine's, let myself in – left it on the latch like arranged – dump my coat and bag by the door.

'It's all right, Nanny's at knitting club,' Sabine shouts from the bedroom, her familiar sprayed White Musk making its way to me.

'How did ya manage to get out of class,' I call back.

'Sure, it's terrible so it is, I had to leave after second class, fucking horrendous period cramps so I have.' She enters the living room, mock doubled over, hands clenched to her stomach.

'Jaysus, and you should have seen the face on Mr Greene. The second I mentioned the rag, he was signing me out quicker than hot snot so he was,' she laughs.

I sit myself at the table; she pulls out the chair beside me. I reach into my inside pocket, unfold Da's letter again, the folds reinforced with each reopening. I push it towards her and she takes it in her hands, not sure of what it is, or what it contains, but it doesn't take long for the recognition to drop, the prison watermark strengthening in the light.

'So you opened one,' she says eventually, filling the heavy silence between us. 'I never actually thought you'd open one.' She lets her words hang there. I'm not really sure how to respond, because I never thought that I would ever open one either. Her and Ma have been at me long enough to do it; Sabine even went as far as retrieving one from the bin, said she'd read it for me if I wanted, let me know what was in it. But the full force of me saying no stopped her from ever trying again, or from ever even mentioning it. Here I was like a hypocrite, passing her the very letter I told her to fuck right off from, that I barricaded her away from, and she doesn't even flinch, or tell me where the fuck to go.

'Do you want to see him?'

I push myself out of the chair and begin to pace. Sabine stays where she is and rereads Da's words, heavy etched in blue Bic, the pencilled first draft still visible underneath.

'Do you?' she asks again, her steadiness, her strength, filling the room.

'Ah Sabine, I don't know.' I rub my hand over my face, the stubble scratching my palm. I rub it again, harder this time, making sure I feel the stab, the pain of it scratching deeper.

'You know I'll go with you,' she says, 'you know that yeah,' and I know that yeah. 'He talks about him a lot,' she says, her eyes back on the letter, the paralleled crease between her eyebrows deepening as she reads on. 'It must have been so hard for him, not being there,' I can hear the crack, 'not being there in the end,' she continues.

'That's on him,' I say, 'all fucking him. He had to go and involve himself, get involved in it. He could have said no. He could have walked away, told them all to go to fuck.' I kick the side of the couch; Sabine comes and stands behind me, her vanilla-scented hair brushing my arms, back, her arms on my shoulders, and then right around, enveloping me with the whole of her, always with the whole of her, pressed in extra tight.

'I think you should go,' she says, whispering into the back of my neck, and I lean back into her, close my eyes, wish I could just see things the way that she does, or feel things the way that she does, without all my shades of darkness kaleidoscoping, slicing right through.

Finn

I woke up in the night, all sweating in the bed, thinking that the pyjamas maybe were better left off, and the smell from the room was like Jasmine's lotion, the one she got when she first pierced her ears, and had to rub it right onto the back so they wouldn't get infected and it spilt all over her school trousers and they stank for a week, until laundry day Friday, and that smell was all over the place here. I couldn't help thinking that they were just all too late, to stop an infection with that strong-smelling lotion, because infected I already was.

I was about to get up when I heard them whispering, Ma and Da. The glow from the hall had lit them right up, on the chair by my side, with Ma curled up on Da's knee, whispering into his neck and his ear. I stayed still where I was, because I didn't want them to know I was awake, or to know that I was spying on them, and sure it was nice to see them like that.

'Do ya remember the time when he got at your nail varnish?' Da said, and it was barely a whisper, him trying not to wake me, me trying harder to hear. And Ma's laugh cut right through the forced silence. A laugh that always made you want to laugh yourself, with her head thrown back and mouth so wide you could see right to her tonsils. I tried extra hard not to smile, not to give the game away.

'My good stuff too. Brand new and bright red at that, and he had everything bleedin' covered so he did.'

'And the red all over his hands, and his face, and his hair,' said Da, 'swearing it wasn't him.' Now Da was laughing too, being a little less careful to hide the volume of him. 'Jaysus, it was hard to keep a straight face through the strict that day,' he said, shaking his head, squeezing into Ma.

'Or the time when Nanny Peg's brush broke and her sweeping the floor.'

'And out he comes with *ah fuck, Nanny*, and me Ma pulled the ear off me for teaching the young ones bad language,' said Ma, and Da was rightly laughing now. 'And the time he brought that mangy cat home, the one he found out the back by the bins.'

'And the eye gone on him.'

'And the fleas hoppin' off him.'

'But you let him stay,' Ma said, 'you took him to the vet and all, do ya remember?'

'Jaysus, yeah, and he nearly scratched the bollox off him, some poor young lad, just doing his training.'

'And you put a box by his bed.'

'With the bedding from his old cot.'

'Fuck, I could never say no to Finn.' They were not laughing any more. It had gone back to being quiet, and smelling of lotion that was just trying too hard to conceal.

'Will he be all right, Annie,' I heard him whisper.

'I really don't know, love,' said Ma, winding her arms tighter now, everything wrapped around him, encasing him, securing him, with all that she was and all that she had. I think he was crying now too. Big gulps into the dark and the silence. Breaking it apart.

I wanted to let him know that I was awake. To tell him that I was OK. To promise that all would be fine, he'd see.

But I didn't.

I couldn't.

Sure Da wouldn't want me to know that he cries.

Joe

It didn't take much to arrange, a lot easier than I thought it would be. I was on his visitation list, which meant it could be scheduled, just like that. I picked Tuesday, the very next day, just in case I'd lose my nerve; even now, as I'm in the communal waiting area, kids hide-and-seeking, babies squalling, Mas ignoring, Radio One's background murmurings, I'm still thinking of getting out, making the great escape. But they have my phone, my wallet, and I was already searched and told the rules, the regulations, so I may as well stay and listen to what he has to say. Shouldn't I?

I didn't tell Ma where I was going. I didn't want her to be thinking that this actually meant something, sure she'd just want me going in with her every week then, and I didn't think I'd be able to handle all of that shite. This once, I told myself. Just this. That's all he deserves. More than he fucking deserves.

The waiting is taking longer than I thought. The tick of the clock on the calming salmon-painted walls beating into my thoughts, dissecting them, leaving them there for me to examine on fucking duplication and I keep coming back to that letter. I should never have opened it. I should never have kept it in the first place; once opened my eyes scanned, and all I could see was you. *Finn. Finney boy. My Finn.* But

123

he was never Da's Finn. Never. His reminiscing and remembering's all warped. All fucking wrong. Memories smelling of roses, masking the decay of reality, because Da wasn't there to see it. Left Ma and myself to that all by ourselves, as if anything else was fucking new, Da never ever failing to surprise, self-fulfilling his own prophecy with ease. We were well used to all of that. Myself, and Ma, and Finn, always well fucking used to that.

I shift in my chair, rub at my lower back, at the puncture mark that was supposed to save your life, and observe the painstaking care taken to make this place just like any average, ordinary waiting room. Mustard and teal couches, safari-themed bean bags, a water cooler, *Ideal Homes* and *Country Livings* fan-spread on a see-through glass coffee table, little handprints smudged, not yet wiped from this morning's eager visitors. But no amount of IKEA soft furnishings could mask the armed guards by the thick, locked steel doors, or the beep of the metal detector welcoming your arrival, or the plastic-gloved pat-down, searching for anything and everything that could be perceived or imagined into any form of weapon.

My name is called and I'm escorted in through the doors and left waiting in a cubicle, with a sheet of bulletproof Perspex shielding us from any form of physical contact, dissolving that awkwardness at least.

He's brought in chained at his feet, but not his hands, and as he sits in front of me, the shock of it, seeing him, looking back at me with Finn's eyes, nearly sends me right out that door. I'd forgotten how much of him was in Finn. But I stay rooted to where I am, stay seated, glaring at him, waiting, only picking up the phone after he does. Daring him to make the first move.

Finn

Dr Kennedy was in today, letting me know the story with my treatment plan. He was the head doctor, apparently, head of my team, but I didn't really know what to make of him, not much to be fair, because I told him my favourite joke and I don't think he knew how to laugh. He had the most boring voice ever, and sure I was more than half zoned out, like a zombie, or something that needed no brain. I wondered if he had any kids like me, if he ever had any fun with them, or was it just that being around the cancer zapped you and everyone around you of having fun ever again?

'Right so Finn, would you like me to discuss your treatment plan with you on your own, or would you prefer that your parents were here too?' He'd been waffling on at me for ages. I wanted to watch *Tipping Point*, and it was on in five minutes, and I hoped that he wasn't going to be still going on about stuff then.

'Ah on my own is grand, Doctor,' I said, and hoped that he would just hurry the feck up.

'Oh. Just great. I find that's the best usually, it means you can ask the questions you might be afraid to ask if they were here.' Sure what was he going on about now? Why did he think I'd be afraid to ask questions around Ma and Da?

'I have already spoken to them both, of course, but sometimes patients want their parents here for this bit too,' and maybe I should have had them here, maybe I needed them here; I was panicking now, if I'd made the right choice.

'Is it OK if I begin now, Finn?' he said, and I started to think that him having a boring voice was not so bad; it made me quiet, and calm, and forget the worry of asking the right questions – well, for now anyway. I nodded my head, not wanting to interrupt him, wanting to listen, and see what he could do about this cancer.

'OK. Well, AML, the cancer that you have, as you know affects both your blood and your bone marrow. We are going to attack this cancer in two different ways.' I started to like him, even just a little bit then.

'Attack?'

'Yes, Finn. The first thing we want to do is to kill the leukaemia cells that are in your blood and your bone marrow now. Then after that is done, we will attack and try to kill any more that may be hiding, or that may not be too strong yet.'

'How will you kill them?' I asked, now getting a bit more curious, warming up to the idea of killing this leukaemia that was taking hold of not just me, but the whole family. I didn't know that they would be attacked, that they would be killed, that they would be able to do any of that.

'We'll do it in a number of ways. First, we'll start with some chemotherapy, do you know what that is?' I shook my head no.

'Well, chemotherapy uses drugs to stop the cancer cells growing, stops them trying to spread. We will be starting yours straight away. Firstly by using a drip, through an injection into your vein, that will get it straight into your bloodstream, and then I am hoping that we can start it by mouth, which is just a tablet, that you will be able to take from home.'

'You mean I'll get to go home?'

'Oh yes, we are hoping you'll get to go home tomorrow, Finn, and then you need to come back once a week for your chemo, for about six weeks, and then, if in remission, that means if all the cancer is gone, you will be able to take it at home then, just to make sure that it doesn't come back.'

'Do I get to go back to school?'

'Yes, there is nothing stopping you going back, as long as you feel up to it.'

'Oh, I definitely feel up to it,' I said, and there I was think-ing that the cancer would mean I had to stay in hospital, or be really sick, or any of those things. 'What if the cancer doesn't all die, what if some of it gets away?'

'We're really hoping that the chemo will get it all, but if it doesn't, we will most definitely do a bone marrow trans-plant.' Even the sound of that word flashed the big needle in front of my eyes again, but Dr Kennedy continued on. 'That's when we take out the bad bone marrow from you, and swap it with some healthy bone marrow from a donor.'

'A donor, what's that?' I didn't think it was like the kebab you got in town.

'A donor is somebody who gives, but they have to be an exact match – usually it's a relative, but we've already tested, and Joe is a match, if we need to use it.' I couldn't think about Joe having to get that injection too. That he would have to do that for me.

'Is my hair going to fall out?' I asked, suddenly remembering.

'Probably, Finn, and your eyebrows and eyelashes too. It's an effect of the chemo, because it is such a strong drug. It could make you feel sick, or throw up, or feel very tired too, or it could do none of these things – everybody is different in how they respond.'

I was getting braver, getting ready to ask the questions that I really wanted to ask.

'Can I give the cancer to someone, if I hug them, or anything like that?' Dr Kennedy's face softened, into a bit of a smile, well, what looked like a smile, for him. Softened.

'No, son, you can't give it to anyone.'

'What if I did blood brothers, could I give it to them then?'

'Absolutely not, Finn, you can't catch it off someone.'

'Then how did I catch it so?' And I tried not to let him see me cry, choked it back, tried to stay strong.

'Son, nobody knows that for sure. But I am telling you this, one hundred per cent, nothing you did caused any of this. There is absolutely nothing at all you could have done to prevent it. Do you understand? That is really, really important.'

I nodded my head again, worked myself up to ask the big one. The question I knew I shouldn't ask, because of Ma screaming no, shutting me off every single time that I tried. I knew then why he said it was better that I talked to him on my own, because I never could have asked it with anyone else there.

'Will I die?' It came out of my mouth, just like that, and I thought I couldn't do it, or say it, I thought I would hide from it, or that he would too, but he didn't. He looked me straight in the face, no hiding or trying.

'I don't know, Finn. But what I do know is that the cancer hasn't spread to anywhere else in your body, which is a really good sign. I'll tell you something else: it is my job, it is your team's job, to do the very, very best that we can to make sure that that does not happen. I can absolutely promise you that.' I believed him. He was honest. He didn't try to shush me, or lie to me, or treat me like I wasn't worth telling.

We were interrupted by the loud ringing of a bell. It was a handbell too, I knew it was, because we had to use it in school when the one through the speaker was broken. Dr Kennedy was really smiling then; he asked me to come and see. We got out into the corridor, right beside where the door to the ward was. There was a big crowd of people, and nurses, and doctors, and kids, and parents, and one little girl, definitely younger than me, stood up on a chair, ringing the hell out of the bell over the door, pulling on a big white string as hard as she could.

'What's that?' I asked Dr Kennedy.

'That's the *I beat cancer* bell – all the patients ring it when their cancer is gone.' Everyone was standing and cheering and laughing and passing around cake, and I was more determined than ever, that I would be standing on that chair, ringing that bell, no questions at all about that.

Joe

'Howya, Joe,' he says, all gruff and crackled, into the phone. He's looking like shite too, the barbed stubble and gouged creases on him. He scrapes his chair forward, twice, leaning himself in closer, the frame of him too big, spilling over the edge of the seat, the left front leg groaning outwards at the weight of him.

'It's good to see you,' he continues on, still moving himself, trying to get comfortable, me keeping my two feet flat grounded, statue still. 'You're looking good anyways,' he says.

'Ah fuck off, Da,' I say, knowing the cut of me.

'Well, you're fucking looking the dog's bollox compared to me, son,' and we both laugh. Da's good at reeling you in like that, making you feel all comfortable in his presence. Until you're not.

'Carthy's collecting for Dessie now,' I say, going to something familiar, yet outside of me. His face gives nothing away, the way he's trained it to do.

'Is it true, Da. Carthy?' His face still stone-set, masking any way of reading it. I'm moving closer despite myself.

'Look, Dessie knows what he's at, so leave them to it,' he says. 'Seriously, Joe, leave it well the fuck alone. Don't be getting yourself involved in the middle of that,' and the wanting to protect is fucking pathetic; I turn my head to the clock on the wall, counting down the twenty minutes left.

'Wait, are you rolling your eyes at me?' The chair rocks on him as he's shifting closer, his rage now all lopsided. 'You think you wouldn't get sucked into Dessie just like the rest of us,' and he's gripping at the counter in front, the half-moon of his thumb whitening at the pressure of it. 'I was about your age, when it happened to me,' he says, barely a flat whisper; I can hear the grind of his back teeth.

'Da. Don't,' I say, dropping my gaze, trying to disengage, but he continues, in his own trance.

'I'd just been kicked out of another home, the social were on my case, urging me to make it up to the perverted bastards running the place so they'd take me back, and there he was, my knight in fucking shining armour.' He gives a harsh laugh into the phone.

'It started small, a few favours here and there, in return for a place to stay, a safe house back at the flats.' He is itching at his collar now, pulling at it. I fix on that instead of his face.

'I thought it would be easy to stop. I thought it would be so fucking easy to just walk away whenever I wanted, but the more he asked for, the more I gave, the more favour I got, the more fancy shit I could buy, the more up the ladder I climbed,' he is still trying to catch my gaze, 'and the further it was to see the ground.' He places one hand over his eyes, rubbing his thumb against his temple.

'Your Ma,' his hand pushing harder, the counter creaking with him, 'I fucking completely broke her. She had a family, a good one, she had so much laid out for her before I trampled the fuck all over that. Once she was in the picture, he had a hold so tight of me, I suffocated her with it, and here we fucking are.' He's looking right at me now, waiting for me to say something, waiting for me to say anything. But I can't; I just grip the handle of the phone tighter, feeling the tense knot of my knuckles.

'Joe, you've a chance, fucking take it, go to college, get the fuck out of that place and never look back, don't let him fucking take a hold of you like he has me, promise me.' Promise? Him there thinking he has the right to parental advice, that he has the fucking right to anything at all. I hook the phone between my shoulder and ear, clasp my right wrist in the palm of my left, and twist the tight skin around the hard jut of bone, over and back, feeling the burn of it, watching it redden.

'This fucking chair,' he says, turning it over, slapping the bandy leg of it back into position with the palm of his hand, placing it back upright with a slam, it groaning on him again as he sits back down.

'Fuck, Joe, sorry,' he says, running his two hands up over his face, ripples of skin facelifted up and released as his fingers make their way through his hair. 'I didn't want to be getting into any of this,' he leans himself back, a deep sigh caught under his breath, 'just watch your fucking house, yeah,' and I can feel the air around him shifting now, all heavy, and wanting.

'I need to talk about him,' he says. I won't meet his longing. 'Joe, son. I need you to tell me, your Ma just can't,' he says again, and the catch of emotion warbling at his throat, making its way to mine, is too much. Him trying to break me, bleed in under my surfaces, I don't need to tell him shit. About those days, where he was nowhere to be seen. Locked the fuck up. I'm not about to fill in the blanks so he can sleep a little better at night.

'I need to know, how it was for him, in the end,' and his voice is trapped, all ragged and stale. His left hand is on the Perspex now, pressed tight against it, the length of his life-line deep red sprawled there in front of me, and I wonder is it all mapped out, life, before we even get here, life, how it's going to be for us, life, and I look down at my own.

'All this shit, going round in my head, I'm fucking telling you, Joe, it's far worse than anything you could tell me.' He's straightening up, tightening his jaw, bracing himself for me and my truth.

'Nothing,' I say, holding the receiver of that phone so tight that it is throbbing the veins at my wrist. 'Absolutely fucking nothing you have imagined in your head is even close to the reality of watching what happened to him,' I say. 'Knowing that nothing you do will make any fucking difference. Having to just sit there and take it. What the fuck would you know about any of that?' I push my chair, drop the receiver to dangling.

'Joe,' a silent mouth.

'Joe,' a more forceful silent mouth but I'm up and out, not even a second glance given. Not fucking deserved.

I should have known better.

Finn

Back home, and I couldn't wait to see Joe and sleep in my bed, and see all my friends, and go straight back to school, catching up on all the things that I missed. He had the flat all done up, Joe did, with posters, and streamers, and welcome home balloons, and a big 'Miss You' card from school in the centre of the table, with sweets and crisps, and pizzas and Coke. Just like my birthday. But better, because getting to come home was so much more.

'I hope you like it, Finney,' he said. I scoffed into the pizza, horsed it into me after three days of cabbage, mash and ham, or carrots, mash and chicken, or all sorts of other meat and two veg variations, but all tasting the same anyway.

'You not having any?' I asked, and I saw that he just kept looking, like he was afraid to come near. 'You can't catch it, honest,' I said, 'Dr Kennedy promised me that,' and he ran over to give me a hug.

'Don't ever, ever think that I would think that. Ever,' he said, and spun me around till I was dizzy. Nearly sick with the pizza still in me mouth.

'Ah get off,' I said, laughing, spraying a bit of pizza, not meaning to mind. He took up a big slice, and sat down beside me on the couch.

'How come you didn't come in to see me?' I asked, now

that he had stopped staring, now that he was relaxed on the couch. 'I know you were in, Dr Kennedy said you were in to get your bone marrow checked. To see was it a match.' He kept his head down.

'I didn't want to see you in there,' he said after a while. 'It would make it all too real.' He was about to say something else too, but I didn't think I wanted to hear it.

'Well, I'm glad you got to feel the pain of that big fecker of a needle too,' I said, and he started to laugh, relieved to be off the hook.

'Jaysus, the size of that yoke,' he said, 'you'd better not be needing it now, my bone marrow, because that thing hurt like a bitch,' he nudged.

'Well I won't, this chemo thing is going to kill it all, wait till you see,' and a shadow came over him; I couldn't read him like I usually could. I was glad he hadn't come to see me.

The doorbell rang, on, off, on, off, no rest for the wicked like. It was Jasmine, who took a running jump onto the couch, on top of me.

'I thought they'd keep you in for ages,' she said, still not letting go of me. 'Do you not have to stay for ages when you have cancer?' she asked again. I could see Ma wince, and Jasmine's Ma ready to pounce. Jasmine's Ma had a chicken curry in her hand and a bottle of wine, and her and Ma made space for themselves at the table, huddled into their own conversation. Joe was over by the DVD player, putting in *Star Wars*, I think, and Jasmine leaned herself in closer to me.

'Is your hair going to fall out?' she asked, concern all over her face.

'Yeah, probably, and my eyelashes and eyebrows too.' Her look was pure horror, and I busted my hole laughing, then so did she, nearly crying she was laughing so much.

'Jaysus, you're going to look freaky as shit,' she said, 'like one of those alien thingies that you grow in slime.' We were laughing again. And I couldn't wait to get back to school. Back to being me again. Back to being normal.

Joe

'Cheers Annie, ta love,' and I see him there, with a mug in hand, Ma putting out a plate of biscuits, him putting his feet up on the coffee table beside them. Fucking Dessie Murphy, in all his Badger glory.

'Here he is, the prodigal son.' He gives me a wink and takes a big slurp of his tea. 'Come over here to me sure, tell me all the sca.' He's still slurping away, dipping a digestive, sucking the tea out of it before melting it into his mouth. A bit of the crumb is stuck to his moustache and beard; he gives it a good wipe of his arm, the smear of crumb now stuck to his burgundy woollen sleeve instead.

I don't move; I stay where I am at the jamb of the bedroom door.

'Any word on when he might be out,' Ma interrupts, used to defusing tension around me, used to stepping herself in.

'I'm on it, love,' he says, not taking his eyes off me, his dunk and slurp mocking from the couch. 'We've got the loophole now, so any day,' and that's what he does. He knows every technicality, every glitch, every loophole ready to be prised wide open when needed, and he always gets his way. If he wants it.

'But I'll have a word with Joe now, Annie,' his stare still fixed on me. The childhood memories of sweets and money and packets of crisps tinged with the sword-edged cut to him. Everyone knew that there was no such thing as a rumour when it came to Dessie Murphy; what you heard was most definitely what you got.

'Now, Annie.' The boom of his voice echoes the room; he is still sat in the same position, slurping the same tea, wearing the same burgundy machine-knit cardigan, and it's hard to imagine that boom was him at all.

'I'll head into town, get a few bits so.' She grabs her shopping bag from the press. I can see the white clench of her knuckles, the tight set of her jaw, and oh how I know she would love to tell Dessie to fuck the right off.

'That's the girl,' he says, lifting his mug for another slurp.

Ma is standing at his back, looking like she's going to say something, waiting there, about to say something, her mouth half open forming around her invisible words; no one gets away with calling Ma love, or girl, or honey. *It's fucking Annie*, she'd say, but she picks up her purse and pulls the door behind her.

I keep my position at the jamb of the door, keep my arms folded, a barrier between him and me.

'You're very like your Da was at your age, has anyone ever told you that.' He sets his mug and feet down, leans his elbows on his knees, pushes himself forward to get a better look at me. Taking in the Da in me. Hoping for the Da in me. Trying to break into me, and my armour.

'Yeah, well you do,' he says, not waiting for my reply, 'he had the same stubborn prick of a head on him too, so he had.' He lifts his head back, laughing to fuck at himself with his metallic back fillings on show. I just wish he'd get on with it, whatever it is that he came here to say.

'I heard they took you in the other night.' Here we are, straight to the point. I don't say anything at all, don't move, don't flinch, don't give him the satisfaction that I am in the slightest bit concerned about what he does and doesn't know about me. But the palms of my hands are beginning to sweat and a buzzing is starting its low insistent hammering in my ears. He's up now, making his way towards me, placing his hand just over my head, shadowing me with his bulk.

'Lucky you were able to get my gear sold before they came, eh.'

Fucking Carthy and his big fucking mouth. He bends into me now, as close as he can, his sour warm breath all over my face, heating it, making it wilt.

'It was for Sabine,' I say, trying to make myself sound assured, confident, but the shake of nerves cannot be mistaken.

He inches in closer. Saying nothing, but suffocating my personal space, with that bulk, with that sour breath, waiting for me to say something, to reveal something, to trip myself up in my own guilt. I've seen him do this before, watched as his lackeys squirmed under his gaze, pleaded with him, admitted guilt, made excuses for what they did, without him ever having to say one word, all just from the intimidation of his gaze. But I'm not sure what it is he is looking for from me, what trap it is he's hoping I'll fall into.

'To clear her debt,' I say again, a little more confident this time, his gaze still intense, still unfaltering. 'I couldn't be done for anything anyway, I had none on me when I was arrested.' He catches my baby finger, digs pressure right into the nerve of the nail, pushes it right back till he hears it crack, then pushing more, shooting a sharp intense pain right up and down my arm.

'Lesson one, sonny, you never say anything when questioned. Fucking never,' the pure torrent of anger coming off him in waves. 'You should know better than that. Fucking never, hear me, Joe.' I nod, trying not to let him see the agony, trying not to let it show even a little, but the tears now stinging, prickling at my eyes, have another story to tell. He lets go eventually; I pull it back quick, too quick, cradling it into me; he gives a little laugh.

'Don't worry, I'm leaving,' he says, moving away from the door, grunting as he straightens himself back to full height, rubbing his hand at the base of his back. 'Jaysus, getting old. Don't ever get old, Joe, it's a fucking balls.' He walks around to the front door, his mask of joviality firmly back in place.

'You'll need to start thinking carefully, about what you're doing, son.' The reminiscing pleasantries are over just like that.

'You need to start thinking of your Ma, and that girl, Sabine.' I melt back into the frame of the door, letting its splintered edges dig into my spine.

'I can offer you stuff around here that no one else can. I

can make sure you keep the flat, pay the bills,' he says, 'but sure you already know that,' he smirks.

'Your Da knew what to do,' and *where the fuck did that get him*, I want to shout.

'He always knew what was best. For all,' and he opens the door.

'Well, I'll be seeing you, Joe,' he says, nearly all the way out.

'I'll be in the Tavern later, yeah,' and he pulls the door to nearly closed.

'Oh, and I'm the one who'll be fucking telling you when young Sabine's debt is paid,' and he slams it firm, leaving me there, with his threats still fresh in the air.

Finn

In the middle of the floor, sat on the broken wooden stool with a towel around me neck and newspapers spread open at the feet.

'Are ya sure about this now, Finn?' Joe asked again, for about the hundredth time.

'Just get on with it,' I said, 'I'd prefer you to be the one to take it.' Cancer was taking enough of me, thank you very much, and anyway, I always wanted to try Da's clippers. Ma would never let anyone near me with them – 'No one will be shaving those curls off ya,' she said, and no one wanted to push that warning. That's for sure.

'Well, I'll start with a number two, see what ya make of it.'

'Number two? No, feck that, I want it all off, honestly, I want you to do it.' I said it stronger this time, no laugh in there, so he would take me seriously, know that it had to be him. That this was the way that I wanted it. The only way that it could be.

'Right, here we go so,' Joe said, resting his hand first on my shoulder, showing me that it would be OK. I could hear the buzzing start right behind my ear, humming closer and closer to me.

'I think this will do the job,' he said, keeping it tight to my scalp, and cut one big stroke through the middle of my head, and then stopped. Why was he stopping?

'Ha, Finn, sorry bud, I just have to get a look at this.' He came and stood in front of me, admiring his handiwork.

'Jaysus, Finn, the bleedin' state of ya,' he said; he had doubled over on himself, laughing.

'Ah show us,' I said, standing up, going to the mirror over the mantel. He was right. It was going to do the job all right. I looked mad. I had one bald streak, right through the middle, with me black curls either side.

'I look like that clown from *It*,' I said, now laughing with him. Creeping up behind him, with me mad bald streak. 'Come on, finish it off before I change my mind,' I said, hopping back down on the stool, careful not to tip the bockety leg. I closed my eyes as the rest of my hair fell in clumps, sticking to my face, and clothes, and shoes, and landed in piles all around me.

'Right, I'm just going to go over it once more to be sure,' Joe said, feeling around my head with his palm, checking for any telltale little stubs of spikes.

'All right, sir, job done,' Joe said with a bow, while rubbing the hair off me with the brush of his hand. I could hear the key in the door, the forced push of it, the swell of it making it trickier to open. I ran to pull the mat away; sometimes it got stuck, made it harder to get in.

It was Da. The look when he saw me, the hair on the floor and the razor on the stool, still plugged in.

'I asked him, Da, to do it. I should have asked first.' I was talking about his razor, his pride and joy, the one he used monthly to keep his own stubble neat and threatening. He grabbed me by the shoulders and shook me hard.

'What the fuck do you think you're doing,' he said, hurt and anger and something else, fear in his eyes. 'Jesus, look at the state of ya, people are going to start treating you different now, like a fucking invalid, is that what you want.' He pushed me back; I stumbled, not prepared this time, like usual.

'Lay off him, Da,' Joe said, coming up closer, squaring up to him.

'And I suppose it was you who did it, put him up to it?' he said, spitting at Joe, anger now taking over from everything else. 'You realise how you're making him look.' He moved closer to Joe. 'You realise what you've fucking done.' He was right in Joe's face.

'What, Da?' Joe challenged. 'What way have I made him look?'

I wished he hadn't said anything. You should leave Da when he was like this. Joe knew he should be leaving it. But Joe wasn't; he pushed, coming at Da.

'What way have I made him look?' Joe said again, louder this time, him the one getting into Da's face. Da started to back off, a bit.

'Like he has fucking cancer. Is that what you were going to say.' Da has backed off completely now, like the dawning of the cancer has stubbed the anger right out.

'Well, he fucking does have cancer, Da. This is him. This is how he looks now. You and Ma are tiptoeing around it, but he's not. He's ready to fight. Him. This is about him. Not Ma, not me, not fucking you.' He grabbed his coat, and slammed out the door.

Da went into his bedroom. He couldn't look me in the eye. One look at my head, reminding him that I wasn't the same. That something was in me now, that he didn't have any control over.

I shook the towel out from around my shoulders, got the brush from the side of the fridge, and began to sweep up the hair gathered all over the floor, pushing the last of it into neat piles, ready to be discarded into the bin.

Joe

The rain is only hopping and I don't even bother to shield it, let it drip right through. The barflies are out in their droves, blowing the stink of Guinness off of them, not giving a fuck about the rain either, hovering at the door of the Tavern, Fat Mick leaning in for the chat with them, opening the door as I approach, 'Bad one tonight, bud' following as I enter.

I make my way up to the bar, searching for the stool in the centre where I can get myself settled in, where I can watch the goings-on without being fully immersed. Yet. Then I spy her coming from the back room. Fuck.

'I thought you said you were only doing days,' I say, and Pat comes up behind her, the big delighted head on him.

'She just couldn't keep away,' he says, spinning her around the bar, like the cat who caught the fucking cream.

'Ah here, Pat, you're after making me balls up the head of the pint.'

'Sure fuck that, it's only for bleedin' Ned.'

'I heard that and all so I did, ya bollox,' Ned says from the table at the side of the bar, giving himself a perfect view of the match projecting from Pat's new, heavily wall-bolted flat-screen, obstructing all with his chair right in the middle of the lounge. He wheels himself over and pulls at my sleeve, gesturing for me to come down to him.

'But sure, isn't it great to have her back, Joe, really fucking great,' and it is. The shine of her is starting to come back, peeking through the tarnish, but she wasn't supposed to be here, she wasn't supposed to see me with him. Again.

'Now go and bring us me pint, there's a good lad, and make sure she puts a proper head back on it, ah sure tell her to make a fresh one.' He wheels himself back into position.

'You'll take what you're given,' Pat calls after him, placing the pint with the sloppy head in front of him.

'Sure seen as it was pulled by the lovely Annie, I'll let you away with it, just this once mind.'

'Would ya ever fuck off with yourself, Ned, you're not at your auntie's now.'

'Who are ya fucking tellin'.' He takes a big gasping sip of his pint, running his thumb along the frosted condensed sides.

Ma steadies her gaze on my freshly splinted finger, watches it as I shield it close to my chest.

'So, what did he want?' Ma asks, when she is sure Pat is occupied, not wanting to let people know that I could be involved, that I'm projecting or emulating Da, but word is whispering about the place, I can feel the hum of it, word always gets out about the place here.

'Ah nothing, Ma,' I say, but the look on her, pure disappointment, her steady gaze not leaving my finger.

'Well, looks like he meant business whatever it was.' She's nodding at the bandage, her well used to home-job patch-ups, her thinking she was done with having to keep the first-aid box hidden under her side of the bed well stocked.

'Don't,' she says, holding her hand on mine, 'just promise me, don't,' she says again, and is gulping back at the tears that just come easily to her now, that never did before, turns her back to me so she can wipe them away quickly, without me having to see. I shift on the stool, trying to get myself settled, trying to ignore the looks she keeps throwing, trying to ignore the Da in me, creeping right in, making it harder and harder to hide.

Laughs are coming from the snug. Dessie is there, in the middle as usual, Carthy still lingering on the edges. To the outsider all looks casual. It's a great bunch of lads catching up on the realities of life, bitching about the missus or the boss or spreading the goss, just like any flock seen hugging their pints up and down the country. To the outsider. He knows that I'm there, but he won't register or recognise. There's no nod of the head, or wink of the eye, or any acknowledgement needed for him to know that I'm there, or to ever even doubt that I would show up in the first place.

My phone pings on the bar where I've left it; I flinch at the sound of it.

Hey, how's it going? Look, sorry, yeah? I really am, wondering if you wanted to head into town, grab a coffee, drink, head to the cinema, whatever? Let us know, all right?

Fucking Johnny. I delete, and push the phone deep into my pocket.

It's getting busier; I can feel the press of them crowded up around me, shouting their orders up at the bar. I'm closed in, my pint is slowly sipped gone, and the quadruple-Nurofen oblivion for the finger is wearing off and the dull throbbing pain of it is just throbbing harder and he knows it, senses that I'm about to leave, on my last edge of patience, dissects my unease with an 'Are ya not calling in to us, Joe' across the hatch, timing his moment perfectly, as usual. I'm weighing up the options when I catch the face on Carthy, the snitching little bastard, only disgusted that I'm being asked into the inner circle, only shocked that I've made my way in, only sickened to fuck that I'm worming into where he wants to be, without ever having to lick even one hole. He was always like that, ever since we were kids, always wanting what I had; if I'd a new jumper, he'd have his Ma get the same one, if I said I liked fish-finger sandwiches, he'd be going on about how much he loved them too, and no matter where I sat in school, he wanted to be right in there beside me.

'Ah sure, why not,' I call back, and Ma is giving me a look, to sit the fuck back down, the telepathic power of it, willing me to stay the fuck where I was, but putting that little shit Carthy back in his box is just too hard to resist.

I make a right show pushing past him, smirking into his face, daring him to say anything, and he's raging too, so he is, raging to fucking fuck. I can tell by the hold of him.

'Rat,' I whisper into the side of him.

'What did you say?' he says, pulling at the elbow of me, his eyes hollowed open and wide, all pupil and black.

'You heard.' I reef my arm away, giving a quick stamp closer towards him as I do, making him jump a bit, the fright of him, the fear of him still, of me.

'What was all that about,' Dessie says, nodding towards Carthy, as I squeeze myself in beside him.

'Ah nothing much,' I say, but the shock still lingering, clinging to him is making me uncertain, gnawing away at me, unsettling, not so sure it was him who ratted me out after all.

'Annie, another pint here for Joe.' He turns himself back to me, catching me in my unease, taking it in, absolutely revelling in it, keeping me how he likes it, unsteady, all kept on the back foot.

'Your Da is doing well,' he says. I'm not sure what it is I'm supposed to say, not sure of what is expected of me, so I don't say anything, just sip at the pint in front of me, slammed down by Ma, her expression pleading with me to just go home.

'But he's starting to get a bit soft, your Finn has started to scoop at the hardness of him,' he says, and I grip my pint harder at the mention of his name, at the power of it, that I can still be shocked by it, after all these months.

'He says you wouldn't be up for what I'm asking,' he's leaning in tighter to me now, 'but I think he just doesn't want me asking,' he leans back, 'and then there is the matter of young Sabine,' he says, sipping at his own pint now.

'What are ya asking?' I say.

'Aha, so I was right,' he says, clapping me on the back.

'I knew I could count on you, son,' he says, his hand now gripping on my neck.

'What are ya asking?' I say again, and he laughs at that.

'Well, Finney certainly didn't suck the hardness out of you.' He sips away again. I wait until he's ready, keep the silence there between us until he fills it.

'One of our runners let us down, we need a new face for a job this Friday.' I still keep to myself, don't give anything away.

'We need someone fresh, see, someone they won't expect, it'll take just a few minutes of your time – leave a package for one of our lads, your Sabine fully off the hook, and maybe a few bob for yourself too, all going well.' I look at him then, he gives me a wink, and I think of all the bills piling, and the final notices unopened, and the rent that is due, and Sabine. Sabine's debt completely paid.

'So, are ya in,' he asks, looking like he's not too bothered by my response, looking like he doesn't really care which way I go.

'A one-time thing,' I say finally.

'I suppose it could be,' he says, looking straight at me, both of us knowing that it just isn't true, 'if you want it to be,' he says, keeping his stare right there.

'A one-time thing,' I say again, finally, firmly.

'All right so, a one-time thing,' he glints, then moves himself away, slapping the table in front of him with 'Another round there, Annie,' Ma doing her best to keep up, to stay in her place and not to kick the fucking Badger's den, but the grip of her hand on the pump at the bar tells me I'll be hearing it all from her later. As another pint is placed in front of me, Dessie leans himself in closer, right into my ear, every inch of stale beer and smoke suppressing my space.

'Never forget, Joe, I always protect my own.' He buys me another drink, and another, and I'd forgotten how much fun 'Uncle Dessie' is, and I ignore the looks that Ma is giving, and I take the drinks that I'm being given, and maybe slipping into Da's mould wouldn't be so bad after all.

Finn

We went in on the bus, Joe and me, and stopped in for a chip butty in the Abrakebabra first, right next door. 'God knows what shite they'll be giving you in here,' Joe said, as I squeezed extra tomato sauce on mine. Ma wanted to come, and Da too, seeing as it was my first one, but there was work with Ma, and business with Da, and sure there would be loads more, I told them, five, so they said, one a week.

Joe took me out early from school and everything. For a minute I thought Mrs O'Sullivan was going to give me a hug on the way out the door – thank Jaysus she didn't, scarlet for me that like, there in front of everyone – but she settled for a pat on the back, even though she knew I'd be back in tomorrow. I hoped she wouldn't be doing it every week like, making a big deal out of it.

We went in through the hospital sliding doors, gassed by a cloud of smoke as we entered, the seasoned smokers all hacking away, not a bother to them like, and went straight up to the ward. Joe had been told where to go, no waiting around for us, fancy VIPs we were. Nurse Sarah was already there and Dr Kennedy, all business-like, ready to go.

'Hello, Finn son, we'll get you set up in a jiffy,' *in a jiffy*, and I tried to catch Joe's eye; who the hell said *in a jiffy*, Dr Kennedy, that's who.

'Right, Finn, we'll just take a blood sample first, make sure we're all ready to go, that there are no extra viruses in there,' and he must have seen the panic, 'it should be fine, son, you've been feeling OK? No coughs or sniffles or anything like that?'

'No, all has been grand, Doctor,' Joe answered for me. The seriousness on his face, the concentration, the drinking of it all in, started to scare me.

'I'm just going to put a little line in here, Finn, right there in the fold of your arm.' It tickled when he pressed on it, and Joe moved in closer, stood at the other side of me.

'We'll keep it in, this little tube thing here, so try to mind it if you can, it means we don't have to keep redoing it at every visit.' He started squeezing my arm, tight, helping the veins to pop right out.

'Just a little scratch now,' and he had it in, and taped, and bandaged into place and two lots of blood already taken, just like that. It was already starting to itch, the place where he'd stuck it, the little tube. I wasn't sure I liked the idea of it hanging out of me like that, all the time. What would happen to it when I went swimming, or what if it got knocked out in a tackle, or if it got caught on the sleeve of my Dublin jersey on match day? If it was reefed out of me, would that do even more damage to my blood?

'Right, I'll just get this tested, then we'll order up your chemo cocktail and we'll be good to go.' He was out the door, with my two bloody capsules.

I was told I could leave for a bit, take a look around, go to the shop, but I didn't do any of those things. Instead I inspected the ward I was in and this time I wasn't on my own; the room was full with kids like me, some in the beds, some in chairs, some with curtains closed around them tight, blocking. All with headphones in, iPads being played and parents fussing around them, being completely ignored. Joe tried not to look too hard at the others, I could see him taking quick sideways glances, but I couldn't get enough. I took in those with bandanas, those without, those with tubes in their nose, and I wanted to ask them everything.

'Your first time,' a boy about my age asked, a blue and black bandana tied around his head, barely looking up from his Nintendo DS.

'Yeah, yours,' I said, and immediately felt like an idiot, obviously it wasn't his first time.

'Ha, no. I'm on round two,' and he put the DS down, 'prevention this time I'm told,' and some of the others rolled their eyes at this. 'I'm Michael by the way.'

'Finn,' I answered back.

'Well, Finn, make sure they give you the sick meds, helps a lot after, stops you puking like a scene from *The Exorcist*.' A few laughed and nodded at that and Michael stuck back in his headphones, signalling that our conversation was over. Not wanting to make friends, or make small chat, or do anything at all really.

'Don't be too upset,' and Nurse Sarah was back at my side, 'most here just want to get in and out,' but sure it made sense, why would you want to make friends with someone who might not be there, or stick around, or die. I looked to Joe; he was still right there beside me. He put a hand on my shoulder, gave it the lightest of squeezes. Sure who needed chemo boy when I had Joe anyway.

'So, I've the biggest decision of all now to be placing on you – would you like the bed, or the chair?' Nurse Sarah asked, her two hands out, surfing her body in between the two, a big smile on her face. It took me a while to cop she meant for the chemo.

'Oh the chair, definitely,' I said, no way was I lying in the bed like a bleedin' auld lad or something.

'Great choice, sir,' she said, and propped up some pillows on the back of the armchair. 'Right so, get yourself settled in there now,' Sarah said, and I hopped into the chair. Joe hung about awkwardly behind, but close enough to still protect, still see what was going on.

I could see the bag of chemo in Sarah's hand, all ready to go. I'd been told how it would work, knew what to expect, but Joe couldn't hide the fear all over his face, his eyes darting from the bag, to me, to Sarah, back to me. All rapid response like.

'It'll be about four hours today, love,' said Sarah, as she hooked the bag up to my line. 'But you can wheel yourself around, see, like this,' and she showed me how the bag moved, on a big coat stand with wheels.

'Jaysus, four hours,' Joe said, once she had left, 'we should have brought some stuff with us, downloaded a few movies, brought snacks. Four bleedin' hours.' He started pacing up and down.

'Ah sure it's grand, don't I have you to talk to.'

'For four hours.' He was getting pissed off.

'And sure you can go to the shop and get me stuff, you know, because I have the cancer and all.' I made my eyes really wide, and tried to make them well up for extra effect.

'Fuck off. You've got cancer? Since fucking when?' And we busted our holes.

'So will ya go to the shop,' I asked, pushing my luck again.

'Arra, go on so, what do you want?'

'A Slush Puppie. And get a mix of flavours, blue, red and brown, but don't let them mix it, I want to see the stripes.'

'You contrary little bastard,' Joe laughed, but he went to get it all the same.

Joe

I'm trying to be all quiet, yeah, but the drink in me, the buzz of it, is making it harder than required. I tried phoning, but she had it turned off, so here I am at her bedroom window, curtains shut tight, trying to get her to answer the door.

'Sabine,' I whisper again, in between fits of giggles. My knocking is getting louder and her face is at the window, all haunted black, and the click of the door has her in front of me.

'What the fuck, Joe.' I pull at her hand, bring her with me, to the roof of the flats, and we look over the lights of our city. 'You're fucking mental, you are,' she says, but gives me a punch in the arm. I catch her hand and entwine it in mine.

'And you're fucking magic.' I turn her hand to kiss the inside of her wrist.

'You're locked,' she says, taking her hand back and clasping them between her shivering knees.

'Sorry. Yeah, sorry.' I go to give her my coat, to stop the shivers of her, but then remember I left it in the Tavern and I start to take off my T-shirt instead.

'Fuck, Joe.' She stands up, arm grasped around herself, bouncing up and down on the spot. I can't get the shirt over my head, I'm stuck; I lie flat on my back stuck to shit, one arm in, one arm out, all hokey-cokeying myself.

'Look, is there something you wanted,' she asks, cutting through my dilemma.

'Sorry, Sabine,' I say again, get myself up, leave the T-shirt twisted as it is, 'sorry, I am, sorry.' But her arms are still tight, shielded against me.

'It's three in the morning, Joe, what do you fucking want?' I think it's the first time that I'm properly drunk. I love the courage, the electricity that it gives me; like I'm on top of the fucking world. I need to explain, to let her know. I move closer, but I'm stumbling, and the blur of her is starting to multiply, making her harder to reach.

'Jesus, who the fuck got you into this state?' It's more to herself I think than it is to me, but I need to tell her. Tell her what I came here to do.

'I've sorted things with The Badger,' I say, coming up to her, expecting her to see, expecting her to realise what I'm starting to see and realise myself.

'Sorry,' she says.

'The Badger, it's all sorted. No more hassling, for you or Ma.'

'Seriously, Joe, what the fuck are you on about,' and the bounce of her is gone, the heat of her anger putting a right stop to that.

'Ah don't be like that,' I say, moving closer. 'I did it for us, for Ma.' I try to move closer again, testing the waters, seeing if she'll let me in.

'Joe, don't tell me you're mixing with fucking Murphy.' She is starting to pace now, in small laps right in front of me, making the blur of her intensify.

'He's not really that bad, Sabine, and it's just something small, a favour is all, just once like.' She stops her pacing, arms soldier-straight, fisted at her side, and looks directly at me.

'Don't. Just fucking don't. It's Murphy. Do you think he gives a shit about me, or your Ma, or fucking you.' She comes right up, points at me right in the ribs. 'He doesn't give a shit about anyone but himself, Joe,' and she turns to go.

'Please, don't be like that.' I hold her, lean into her.

'No, Joe. No. This isn't you. It's not. Don't you fucking kid yourself that this is because of me or your Ma,' and she's gone, leaving me to my inevitability that I'm just sick and tired of fighting any more.

Finn

Well, chemo boy was definitely right about one thing: I should have asked for the sick meds after the first session, puke was most definitely involved – a lot of it. Number two took my eyelashes and brows, and that was worse than the puke, but I was just finished number three, halfway there, and it hadn't been that bad at all really, I was now starting to become a pro.

I knocked in for Jasmine. I was still not used to the grimace her Ma gave me when she opened the door, looking at me like I was some sort of freak. That I would somehow break apart at any given second. She didn't know what to say to me either, which was so strange – she had known me since I was a baby, we had the photos in Ma's old brown album with the sticky clear plastic over each one to prove it. *I'm still me*, I wanted to say, *nothing has changed*, I wanted to scream. *I am still exactly the same.*

It was funny how my cancer made other people change. I could see it at school too. With people who I thought were my friends, who now kept their distance, not knowing what to do around me. Afraid that if they played with me, they'd make my cancer worse, or maybe even catch it themselves. Worse than even that, some of the kids who hated my guts, like Billy bloody Redmond, would now hover around me because their Mas said they should feel sorry for me. Offering to carry my bag, running to hand my copy up to teacher, giving me their best sandwich in their lunchbox, but still keeping their chocolate biscuit for themselves mind. No matter how hard I tried to fit in, be the same, I was now different to them. Principal Kelly even made a big show of greeting me every morning, signalling out my difference, highlighting me in luminous yellow for all to see. I just wanted to be all blended in, like I used to be. Why couldn't anyone let me be me any more?

'You're late,' Jasmine said, grabbing her bag by the door, 'and ya never called in yesterday after either,' she said, but linking my arm with hers all the same. 'Hey, where's your gear? Soccer try-outs are after school, remember.' I did remember, but what was the point in all that, I'd have to miss days with the chemo and all.

'Ah Jasmine, sure everyone knows I'm shite.'

'No, no they don't.' At least she tried to make herself sound even a little bit convincing. She kept it up a bit longer, tried to bump up my confidence, all Jasmine style, and I just couldn't keep the grin from my face.

'Oh, all right then, yeah everyone thinks that, but sure who gives a shit about them, it never stopped ya before,' and I didn't want to tell her the real reason why. I didn't want to be the one who kept bringing chemo back into the conversation. That belonged to Wednesdays, between twelve and four, in the hospital, not out here on The Yard with Jasmine.

'How about I come to cheer you on anyway,' I said, 'be there as your good-luck charm, not that you need it like or anything. I don't even really know what you're so worried about, sure you and I and even Ned's mangy cat knows you'll make the team.'

'But we don't know that, what if I mess up, what if I slip and end up giving an own goal, what if I don't score the most as usual and bloody Fintin McGrath ends up as primary striker,' her bitterness from him taking that crown three years ago still raw.

'Ah here, as if,' and she kept the head down, not wanting to jinx her luck. 'I'll practise some penos with you at break if you like, you know, to warm up that golden boot of yours.' She broke into a grin and gave me a big hug about the shoulders.

'Ha, look, your best friend is out again,' and there at the school gate was Principal Kelly, on the lookout. His face all twisted looking, which I supposed was him trying to be friendly, when he saw me. He even added in a wave. As if it wasn't bad enough. My personal meet-and-greet.

'Jaysus, you think he'd lay off already, is he going to be doing this for the rest of my school life, sure I've only three bloody chemos left.'

Jasmine laughed at my side.

'Good man, Finn, great to see you. Good man.' He stood aside to let me in as if I was the president or something.

'Sir,' I said, keeping the head down.

'No hello for me, sir?' Jasmine asked, smirking away.

'Less of that attitude, Jasmine, unless you'd like to keep us company in my lunchtime detention this afternoon,' said Kelly, his bushed eyebrows knitting together in annoyance.

'Sorry, sir,' Jasmine said, keeping her head down next to mine. 'Dick,' she whispered, but only after giving a good glance over her shoulder to make sure Kelly wasn't in earshot. Not too impressed that her link to me didn't give her automatic freedom of speech like she thought.

'Listen, I didn't get the homework done last night, so I'm just going to say I was around at yours, yeah, helping you get over the chemo.' I couldn't help but laugh.

'She's on to you, Jasmine, you say that every week.'

'She's only on to me because you keep doing yours. Like what's the point in having cancer if you're not going to milk the perks, that's what I say.'

We really laughed then. Maybe she had a point.

Joe

The head on me when I wake up. I squint myself into the brightness of the kitchen, run the tap and drink right there from the spout. I rummage around in the top press, searching for any kind of painkiller that will put an end to the ceaseless fucking hammering.

'Good night so?' Ma asks, her face all fuming, arms all folded. I'm flashed back to Sabine when I made a complete and utter tit of myself, and my head just hammers harder.

'Ah Ma, don't, I'm bleedin' dying.' I lie on the couch, close my eyes and try not to move a muscle, each twitch a sharp dart into my brain and behind my eyes.

'Up with ya,' she says, hitting at the ends of my feet.

'Ma, seriously, just leave us a while, yeah.'

'I said fucking up.' She is at me again, pulling at me, to get me the fuck up. I slowly inch myself into sitting, keeping the pressure on the head with my two palms pressed in deep, to stop it busting right on out. I make myself open the eyes that I know are rightly hanging out of my head.

'What the fuck are ya doing sniffing around Murphy,' she says, navigating the ground in front of me, her hands wringing around each other, slipping on and off the dulled gold band of her wedding ring finger, twisting it around and twisting it again.

'Don't be worrying, Ma, I know what I'm doing.'

'But you don't, that's the fucking point, Joe. You haven't a clue how he works, how he operates, Jesus, I can't have you mixing yourself into any of this shit too,' and her fingers are rubbing at her temples now.

'Ma, no, honestly, I'm not.' I have to try to make her see, that it's not as bad as she thinks it is, that I won't be owned like Da was, that it will be different for me. 'I know what I'm doing,' I say again, making myself get up, making myself go to her, to try to make her see.

'No, Joe, no. I fucking watched on as he did it to your Da,' she says, 'well to absolute fuck if you think I'm letting him do it to you too.' She grabs her bag, but it hovers before getting to her shoulder. 'And, school?' she says, her voice wavering but still steel-laced. 'Where does it feature in this grand plan of yours.' Her arms are folded again, tight towards me.

'Ah Ma, don't,' I say, sitting myself back into the couch, letting the soft support of it cushion the thump of my skull.

'Don't, what?' she says, getting herself closer. 'Ask why you haven't gone back, ask why you're determined to throw your life away,' her hands are out of their fold now and clasped together, palm to palm, fingers to fingers, as if in prayer, held at her nose.

'Look,' she says, sitting herself on the edge of the couch beside me. 'I didn't say anything after the suspension.' I close my eyes, not wanting to be part of this, just concentrate on the comfort of the infinite eyelid blackness.

'But you still haven't gone back, and it's been over a week.' She has her hand on my knee now, just for a second.

'Mr Broderick, he wants to help,' she says, 'honestly, he does, he's even offered to call here at weekends, for grinds, to help you catch up.' I sit myself up straighter, look right at her.

'So, what do you think?' she says, her hands back to pleading again.

'No,' I say.

'No?'

'Yeah, no, I'm not going back,' I say, standing despite the pain shooting through the tip of my head, holding my ground, firm.

'Not going back?' she says, her turn to stand now too, facing me off. 'You entitled little prick,' she says. 'What I wouldn't have given for . . .' and she trails off. 'And for what? Fucking Dessie Murphy.' She throws her laugh at me, swinging her bag higher on her shoulder.

'I'm late for work,' she says, pounding her path to the door, Sabine there on her way out.

'Ah howya, love, listen, do us a favour and see can ya knock any sense into that bleedin' son of mine,' and she's gone.

'She's right you know.' She's standing at the door, taking me in, looking at me with something that I have never seen before, and I think it could be fear, there's something familiar in the catch of her, the way Ma used to stand sometimes with Da, and that is the one fucking thing that I never ever wanted to see in her.

Finn

Feeling sick again, it was always worse at night. My head was really busted and me stomach was in bits, and tomorrow was a long way off when you felt like absolute crap.

Lying now, eyes opened, staring up at the glow-in-the-dark stars Joe put up about the place to liven it up, so he said. Lying there trying to decide should I make my way to the bathroom, or would it pass, or if I moved at all would it make it worse, that maybe if I stayed really still the shooting pains running up and down my legs and arms would stop.

Ma was still up, I could hear the TV, and the kettle was on making herself another cuppa, to keep her awake. I didn't know if she slept at all any more; she was always there when I woke up, or if I found it too hard to make it to the bathroom on my own. I didn't want her to worry, or fuss, but it would be nice to sit with her for a bit.

I made my decision and swung my legs over the rail, made some attempt at getting up, but that just made it worse, the sting of the movement, the brush of the sheet sending a flame of heat right through my body. I wasn't too sure I could do this now. I leaned back towards the bed, half in, half out, trying to make up me mind like, not quite sure of it.

I was just about to get back in, decided to just stay put, give Ma the night off and not be fretting her as usual, when I heard the bang on the door.

'Annie.'

The door was still banging. It was Da shouting; Joe was up and at the window.

'Get back into the bed, Finn,' he said, opening the bedroom door a crack, not going fully out. I pushed myself to the side of the rail again, this time unable to hide the pain from my face, or my voice, the quick movements pushing me over the edge.

'Jesus, Finn, you OK?' Joe said, coming over now, trying to help, but his hands on my shoulder just made it worse. Pushed the pain further in.

'Help me out, I want to see what's going on,' I said.

'I don't know, Finn, I don't think you should.'

'Help me out,' I said while turning myself over, trying to get my legs to the rail, missing the rungs in the dark. 'Gentle,' I said, as Joe put his arms around me, guided me to the ladder, letting me do the rest myself. Knowing that I didn't want to be treated like a baby, or an invalid, or that I was different, or that I had changed, or that I would never be the same again.

We both got to the door now, and Ma had let Da in; he was pacing, asking for me, and Ma was trying to get out of him what the hell was going on.

'Finney,' he was shouting now, making his way closer to our door. Joe stood in front of me, protecting, arm at my chest, blocking him from me, me from him.

'Wait, Frank. Don't. Tell me what it is, tell me what's going on,' Ma said, trying to get him back, away from the door.

'I don't have long, Annie, let me see him. I want to talk to him first.' Ma ran, her back now concealing our view, covering the crack in the door.

'I'm not letting you near until you tell me,' and Ma was filling the room now, with the voice of her.

'He was undercover, Annie,' he said, 'fucking undercover,' and he held on to her, pleaded with her. 'They know it was me, they'll be here soon, I won't be getting out of this one, not this time.' Ma's shoulders dropped, her hand loosened on the handle, and she pushed Da in the chest, moved herself closer to him.

'Frank, you fucking promised. Promised that you were finished with this,' still pushing. 'You promised.' She was crying now, her fists were being held by Da, he was trying to get her to look at him. 'How could you do it, you're leaving me. To deal with all this. On my own. On my fucking own, Frank.' He had his arms around her now, she was crying into his chest. I opened the door before Joe had a chance to stop me, I stooped right in under his arm, and Da and Ma pulled me into them.

'I'm sorry, Finney, I am,' he said, and Joe was still at the bedroom door. Just looking, not moving, or making any attempt to join us.

'It wasn't supposed to happen like that,' and Joe let out

a laugh, Da's head locked on him now, like a viper ready to pounce.

'What the fuck's your problem?' Da asked, still holding on to us, but his grip was getting tighter, another shoot of pain, and something else. I closed my eyes, silently pleading with Joe to just stop, stop what he was doing, pushing Da's buttons.

'Well, as long as you're sorry, that's fucking all right so,' he said, still at his position, still not moving. Da made his way over to him, clenched his fists right by his side, his anger pulsing out of the vein at his neck, all targeted at Joe, who still held his position, staring Da out of it, silently daring Da to make his move, which came as a full-forced flick of his head butted into Joe's face. And the gasp of Ma, and the spray of Joe, and the ragged rough breaths of Da while Joe's blood pumped, Da's impression bright and dripping for all to see.

We heard the footsteps in the corridor, the 'Open up, it's the Gardaí,' the barging, full force on the door, and we all watched as Da was pushed to the ground, hands cuffed at his back, dragged from our flat, just like that. Joe moved then, to put an arm around my shoulder, to hold Ma's hand.

That was the last time I ever saw me Da.

Joe

She still hasn't entered fully, still half standing there at the door, the wariness dripping off her, trickling right into the place, into me. That's harder to stomach than the embarrassment of last night, that wariness, that fear, of her not knowing how to just be around me. I'm opening my mouth to say sorry, but it won't mean anything, it won't show any of how I wish it wasn't me who made her feel like that in the first place.

She comes in past me, over to the kettle, taps the side of it with her palm, checking, pulls two mugs from the press, empties the coffee granules straight from the tin and pours the still warmed kettle, handing me my mug.

'Sorry,' I say anyway for something to say, and take a sip from the coffee, putting it straight back down again, the unbearable watering of my mouth and tongue taking everything in me not to retch it back up.

'Ah here, just sit back down would ya.' She starts rummaging in her bag as I make my way back to the couch, sink my head back into the headrest, close my eyes trying not to move. I can hear the clink of glass, the gush of the tap, the clink of metal stirring, and a pint glass is guided into my hand, sprays of fizz splashing up at me, forcing my eyes open to look.

'Alka-Seltzer,' she says, 'he's your only man.' She's staring at me, willing me, and I am holding the glass just barely, away from me; she begins to laugh. 'Trust me, down in one.' She lifts my arm, bringing the glass to my mouth, and I do just that, down it in one.

'Jaysus,' I say, the acidic fizz of it sloshing the stomach but at least I'm not retching, well, not yet.

She comes and sits down beside me then, close but not touching, yet close all the same.

'What is it he wants you to do?' she asks, but it's level and calm. She looks at me then, still close but not touching.

'A run,' I say, barely a whisper.

'A run?' she says. I can feel her tense, see it in her, in the lock of her jaw and the straightening of her back.

'Yeah, a run, a drop,' a little louder this time, a little stronger.

'Joe, seriously, a runner, sure Dessie has runners younger than Finn swarming the place.'

'Not a runner, just a run, one run, a once-off,' but she isn't listening, she's up and pacing again.

'He keeps them young, so he doesn't have to pay them, they'd do it for a fucking Happy Meal, Joe.' Her pacing has stopped now; she's standing firmly in front of me.

'It's a once-off,' I say again. 'One time,' I repeat, but she just sits beside me, places both hands on my leg, the one closest to her.

'Listen to me, Joe, this doesn't make sense.' She brings her hand to my face, trying to get me to turn to her. 'Why does he need you for a run?' Her hand is still resting, right on my cheek, willing me to look at her, the warmth of it, the trust of it, trusting in me and I reach my hand up, to take hold of hers, mine stretched right over, imprinting hers. 'It doesn't make sense,' she says again. I turn to look at her now, wanting to keep her warmth locked in tight.

'A once-off,' I say, and her hand drops right down, leaving mine lingering, ghosted of her touch, her warmth abandoning me, for good.

Finn

Jasmine said it was all over school. That everyone was talking about it. That Da was a murderer, that he shot a Guard. I didn't understand any of this. What it meant. When we would be allowed to see him.

Did they let you visit a murderer? Last time he was in for possession, but he was out in three months, we were allowed to visit once a week. I didn't know if they would let you do that with murder.

I was not even really sure if it was murder at all, and I think that the rumours were all wrong, because Ma said the Guard wasn't dead, that he was just in a coma, and Joe told her it was just as good as, but I wasn't sure if that was really true.

It was self-defence anyway; Da was going to get shot, so he had to shoot first. I told Joe this, but he just walked out of the flat and slammed the door behind him without saying anything. Again.

I tried to find out on the news, even hear a bit on the radio, but Ma was shadowing me constantly and kept turning it off every time she heard it mentioned.

Everyone was in and out of the flat. All morning, all day, all feckin' night. Da's friends, the ones he did jobs for. The ones who were frightened of him. The ones who were frightened now that Da was set up. Frightened that they might be next.

Even Dessie Murphy called in, and Ma told me to go to bed so she could have the chats with him and I could hear her crying, so I could, right through the wall, and I heard Dessie talk about how he would get it sorted, how he had his lawyer on the way in to him now, how he would be home before we knew it. He kept talking about someone just sending a message. A message of what like? All I knew was that Da was in prison, and by the traffic in and out of the flat all day, it was serious this time.

I tried to talk to Joe about it when he came back, but he just kept shutting me out. Not wanting to have anything to do with it, not even a conversation about it.

'He's not fucking worth your time, Finn,' he said, and lay on his bunk and put his headphones in. I didn't even try to share them this time.

Ma told me I had to stay at home, not go to school until things blew over, but that made no sense to me. I wanted to go to school, see what they were saying, find out more about what was going on. Sure nobody here cared what your Da did, or why he was inside, loads didn't even have their Das around, and that fella wasn't even dead. So that proved that Da couldn't even get done for murder.

I wondered, if Ma was stopping me going to school, would she stop me from my chemo too. But I only had one left, and Joe had made me a big countdown and all and thumb-tacked it to the kitchen press, low enough so that I could reach it, and cross off the days myself. Dr Kennedy said I would get to ring the bell and we were going to have a party in the flat and I'd already invited everyone. But we were supposed to get in supplies, goodies, and a big cream cake. I wanted to remind Ma, but I wasn't sure if I should say it at all.

I looked in to check on Joe; he was still there, lying on his bunk. I came nearer, and waited. Still nothing from him. I stayed there, not moving, just standing over him, not sure what to do or say next.

'What the fuck is it?' Joe asked, reefing out his head-phones, staring me out of it.

'Nothing, Joe, just—'

'Come on to fuck, Finn, what is it?' He didn't have the time for me right now, I could see it all over his face.

'Are you taking me to chemo tomorrow?' He swung right out of the bed, kneeled in front of me, his two hands firm on my shoulders.

'That dick is not stopping you from finishing your chemo, do you hear me.' He stayed exactly where he was. 'Do you hear me, Finn.'

'Yeah,' I said, barely a whisper.

'Fuck him, Finn. Seriously. Fuck him,' and his grip tightened. 'We're going to celebrate the shit out of you beating this, and we won't give two fucks of our time or attention thinking about him. Do you hear me.'

And I did. Hear him that is. But I still wished Da could be there too, to see me ring that bell, to see me say goodbye to the cancer for good.

Joe

I'm on the veranda and he's there with his legs outstretched, his back against our door, scrambling up, hitting the back of his head as he heaves himself upright.

'All right, bud,' he says, giving me a half-hearted thump on the arm, all playful like, Carthy and his bagging jeans and desperation. 'Just seeing if ya fancy a pint,' he says, his hands stuffed deep into his pockets, trying to casually lean against the side of the door, one leg crossed over the other.

'You. Want me. To go for a pint. With you?' I say, pulling my keys out, moving myself closer to the door, shouldering him out of the way, him stumbling, the casualness being pushed out of him. 'Don't fucking think so,' I say with a laugh, putting my key in, ready to turn it.

'Right, I'll cut to the fucking chase so,' he says, his fist balling, angling himself diagonally into me, preparing himself for battle. 'Just tell me have you told Dessie.' His breathing has gone all quick, rapid, I can see the little beads of sweat forming at the top of his forehead.

'What are you on about,' I say. His phone starts ring-ing, coming from the inside somewhere, jeans or jacket; he keeps looking, from it, to me, to it again, the sweat beading faster, beginning to trickle. 'Well aren't you going to answer that,' I say, using the opportunity to turn the key to open, him still standing there, a small creep of a smile washing over him, pulling at his sleeve to wipe at the sweat.

'Yeah, Joe, yeah I am.' He starts laughing then, another swipe, over and back, soaking all the drops. 'I'll be seeing ya so,' and he's off, backed away, putting his hand inside his jacket, getting out his phone, nodding at me with a wink before it's answered. Fucking clown.

The door is caught on the letter underneath, the pushing of me ripping the middle of it. I bend down to get it, St Augustine's familiar crest there in the corner, its seethrough window addressed to Mr and Mrs O'Reilly. I rip the rest of it, in half, then half again, and hide it down the bottom of the bin. I get to the fridge, only gasping, a halfdrunk bottle of Lucozade, the original, none of your sports shite, in the door. I grab it, make my way to the couch, feeling the vibration of a text at my thigh. I pull the screen closer, lie myself out the length of the couch, prop a cushion behind the head, and fuck it, the Lucozade's gone all flat.

> Hey, what's the story? Just checking in, thought you'd be back by now, but sure look, if you want a chat, or a meetup, just text us back, yeah. And Joe, sorry for being a prick.

But Johnny wasn't a prick, isn't a prick, he's just someone that I was never supposed to meet. My finger hovers over the delete button, but I hit the home key instead, flinging the phone on the table beside me, it knocking into the brown sealed parcel on the table, *For Joe*, in thick black Sharpie stamped on the front. A good rattle of it gives nothing away, whatever it is padded tight within. I run my fingers down the seam, trying to pull it apart, reach into my pocket for my penknife, flip the blade and open. I can see it through the bubble wrap, the shape of it, and it's in my hands now, shock-cold and lighter than expected. I extend my arm, aim it straight in front of me, a one-time thing yeah, put my finger in at the trigger, pull just a little, not all the way, before dropping it straight back down. I shakenly wrap it back up, bubbles popping as I do, back into its box, and I go and shove it into the back of my wardrobe, hidden well out of sight.

Finn

Dr Kennedy told us to get there early, so he could run some final tests, make sure that we could get the go-ahead for the last treatment.

'It's a wait-and-see game for a little bit after this, Finn,' he had told me for about the tenth time.

'He just has to be sure, love,' Ma had said, but I could see even she was getting pissed off with his reaction. 'Could he not let him fucking enjoy the moment like,' I heard her whispering to Joe, although Ma's whispers always carried, I'm not really sure that she even knew what whispering was.

They let Da phone us today, earlier on, before we left. Me and Ma talked to him, but Joe said he didn't want anything to do with him, and that we shouldn't either. He said it loud enough so that Da probably heard and all.

Joe had a big fight with Ma afterwards, so he did, shouting at Ma, asking her why he was letting Da fuck with my head, or have anything more to do with us. But I wanted to have something to do with him. I needed him, not like Joe. If the truth be told, he never needed him like me and Ma did.

Ma and Joe insisted on staying around for the whole four hours.

'No way are we missing this,' Ma said.

'Can't get rid of us that easily,' said Joe, and piled a stack of comics, and DS games, and fizzy worms, the extra-sour ones, well used to filling the boredom at this stage, we were true pros now, the two of us, in on the secrets of how to survive the four most boring hours of your entire life.

'Right, into your throne, young man,' Sarah ordered. Joe had the pillows already all set up, the way he knew I liked them, and Sarah hooked up my line. The last bag of chemo swinging away. I reached first for the comics that Joe had brought. He always hid a few sketches in between the pages, had them stapled in so they wouldn't fall out. I riffled through them all, it was the first thing I did each time, and put them out around me so I could see them, but I couldn't find any. Maybe he'd forgotten with all the drama with Da. Then I saw it. Stuck in the middle of X-Men, right beside Wolverine, it's one I recognised, one that we have hung up over the fireplace at home, the one Joe drew years ago, with me, about three, sitting on Da's knee. Me pulling at his beard, and him laughing. It's my favourite one, because it's just Da and me, and no one else.

I wanted to give him a hug. I wanted to tell him how much this meant to me, to be able to have Da here, even if just a little, but sure he'd already gone to get my Slush Puppie and Ma was gone to bring up some coffee.

'Well, would you look at that,' Nurse Sarah said, peering over my shoulder.

'Me and Da,' I said, and she nodded.

'Will I get some Blu Tack and stick it up for you, Finn, I

can put it here behind the chair if you'd like?' I just nodded my head again, because I was afraid of the tears spilling if I opened my mouth, even a little, and today was definitely not for crying, not for me anyway. Ma was a different story, she just bawled right there in front of me when she saw it and hugged Joe so tightly when he came back with me Slushie, that I thought it would be melted by the time she let him go. If she ever would.

We all held hands when the last drop of chemo left its bag. We did a countdown and all, although we had to restart it a few times – it's hard to tell when it's fully empty, a few little sneaky drops were clinging themselves to the inside of the bag, hanging on for dear life, the feckers. But we didn't care. We didn't mind starting over at all.

Dr Kennedy came to take out my line and the tube, and the skin all around it was now naked and white and pasty. I itched it, gave it a really good scratch, till it scratched red, not afraid any more that I'd knock it out, now I could get on with my life, could start growing all my hair and eyelashes and eyebrows back so people started treating me normal again, so that people would stop asking me how I was, or what happened me, or avoid me, or look at me with a pain in their face that seemed to be a permanent fixture whenever I was in their presence. Maybe, just may-be, Principal Kelly would leave me alone now, go back to treating me the same as everybody else, being all strict and seeing me for lunchtime detention when I didn't do my homework.

'OK, Finn, you ready,' and Dr Kennedy led me to the bell by the nurses' station. There was a cake on the counter and all the nurses were there, Dr Kennedy, a few of the chemo kids and their parents.

'Right, whenever you're ready you can take it away so,' Dr Kennedy said.

Joe bent down, put me up on his shoulders and walked me over to the bell. Ma had her phone out to take a video; her tears were spilling, and she was not even trying to wipe them away, not even a little. I reached out and grabbed the rope, rang the bell as loud as I could, and the nurses pulled party poppers, and the bell could hardly be heard with the roar of the ward, all laughing and screaming and wishing me well and telling me they never wanted to see me back there again.

And oh how I really wished that that was the way it was going to be for me.

Joe

The landline rings, and I jump at the jolt of it, cause the landline is only ever used by him. I wait until a good five rings because I know it's for me, he'll know Ma's at work. I want him to wonder if I'm even here, and it's only as I'm reaching my hand out that I decide if I'm going to answer it at all.

'Mountjoy Prison, will you accept a call from a Mr Frank O'Reilly?'

'Yes.' I wait until the click and he's through.

'Joe, son, are you there?' And everything is just awkward, I don't know what to say. 'Look, Joe, I don't have long.'

'Good,' I say, not ready for this to be the time that he wants to play happy families, play make-believe.

'You're not to do what he's asking, Dessie that is.' I can hear the bristle of him as he gets straight to the point, he's never able to keep it away for long. 'Joe, whatever he's promised you, you can't trust him.' He's talking faster now, trying to get it all in. 'Do you think he gives a fuck about you, do you think he'll protect you, like he did me.' I hear the crack of a laugh.

'It's just once. For Sabine. I need to clear—' I say.

'Fuck sake, Joe, do you think this job will clear it.' He's laughing all manic and mechanical. I pull the phone closer, feeling the heat of it right against my ear. 'He has you right where he wants you, then it'll be one more job, then one more.' I stick to my bold silence, blocking him and his Da-of-the-year lecturings right out.

'Look.' He's trying to keep it even, trying to keep himself calm, but calm never sits right on Da, it always has a way of sliding right off. 'He's coming in to me later.' I clench my knuckles tighter around the handset. 'Dessie, that is,' and I clench them harder. 'Don't worry, son, I'm going to sort this, I'm going to get you out of it.'

'No, you're fucking not,' I say, each word clipped sharp into the mouthpiece, fuck him, swanning in here, getting me out of it. Fuck him.

'I fucking am,' he says, his words roared into inner ear deafness, the sound of a thump of something hollow accompanying it. 'I am not losing another fucking son,' he says, and I slam the receiver, pulling the phone line out at the wall, plaster crumbling along with it.

/

Ma is there pushing hard at the front door, dropping her shopping right behind me, 'Ah what happened here, love,' as she picks up the phone line, fiddling at it to get it back in.

'Sorry, tripped, Ma.' She holds her look a little too long before getting the Hoover from the corner.

'Here, I'll do that.' I take the accordioned nozzle from her, happy for the white noise of it to take over as she packs away the messages.

'Come here, love,' she says as I'm leaving the Hoover back; she's motioning for me to sit with her at the table, a packet of ginger nuts and two fresh mugs of tea waiting. 'It's not about school, I promise,' and I go to join her, dunk the ginger nut till almost disintegration, and suck on it before it falls.

'I saw David there, at the side of Lidl,' she says, again her look holding.

'And,' I say, not too bothered about Carthy and his Lidl escapades.

'And,' she says, giving a blow and a sip of her tea before continuing, 'he was chatting with one of the Brophys, I think.'

'One of the Brophys,' I say, putting my mug down. 'Are you sure?'

'Pretty sure, yeah,' she says, putting down her own mug now too, 'I think it was one of his young lads, Mark, I think he's called, or Martin, something like that, he used to play football with our . . .' And she turns, taking a big gulp of tea to swallow it away. I reach my hand out and place it on hers. 'Maybe you should have a word with him,' she says, clasping her own hand on top of mine. I pull it back.

'Ma, ah no, I don't know,' and her hand is still there, she's turning it over palm-side now.

'Joe, please, if Dessie finds out, you know . . . we all know what will happen if he's double-jobbing. He wouldn't be that stupid, would he,' and she pushes herself to standing. I stand up to match. 'Just give him a heads up, to watch his fucking back,' she continues.

'Ah Ma, look, that's his fucking problem, isn't it.' I can see the sting of my words on her face.

'This,' she says, pointing her finger into my chest, I can feel the poke of it on my ribs, 'is exactly why you don't go hanging around with Dessie fucking Murphy,' taking her arms and folding them tight tucked into each other, not trusting them, and I can't even look at her. I walk to the couch to pick up my coat.

'Joe?' She just shadows behind me as I make my way to the door. 'Joe, please,' louder now, her fingers gripped right around my arm. I plant my hand on hers, look straight into her eyes, but have to turn away. I will myself to get out the door, close Ma out behind me.

Finn

'You right there so,' Joe called, knocking on the window to hurry us up.

'Jaysus, would you look at him getting his knickers all in a twist,' Jasmine said, filling up her backpack with the last of the popcorn and cans. 'Is he always this bleedin' serious,' and she jammed herself into her red puffer jacket, zipping it right up to her neck. 'He'd need to seriously relax the cacks like, he's up there with Principal Kelly so he is, probably worse – at least you'll get some chat out of Kelly, well, sometimes.' She went on ahead of me and opened the flat door.

It was pissing down, and I didn't even bother with my hood, liked the feeling of my hair wet against my skin and skull again. Stood with my mouth open to let it drop right in.

'Hurry it the fuck up,' Joe called back, powering on ahead of us.

'See what I mean,' Jasmine said, but hurrying all the same; she didn't like the halo of frizz the rain made out of her.

We could see the 11 making its approach, the rattle of its double-deckeredness looking like it could topple with the speed of it.

'Leg it,' Joe said over his shoulder as we all pegged it, all stitched and out of breath as we hopped on and Joe paid our fare. I shook out my hair and ran my hand through it, again, and then again.

'Ah here, what's with the A1 grooming session?'

'Shut it, Jass,' Joe said, holding the pole over my head, and although it had been four weeks since I'd said to feck to the cancer, Joe couldn't get out of that. Protecting. Even if it wasn't needed.

'Well, sorr-eee,' Jasmine said, the huff on her nearly as red as her puffer, and neither spoke again, all the way into town.

The bus stopped right outside Cineworld, and we got ourselves inside. Cineworld was the best; it was so big, and the box office where ya get your tickets was so far away that you got away with paying for just one film, and then you could skive into the rest. You used to be able to nab a few free popcorns too, they had ready-made ones right by the lobby, but they'd moved them all close to the till now, so you just couldn't get away with that any more. But judging by the head on both Joe and Jasmine, it was a one-film day today anyway, if they'd even make it through that.

'We're screen five,' Joe said, and we let him lead the way.

'He's a bit of a prick, your Joe,' Jasmine said, the huff still lingering.

'Ah he's all right, he just doesn't like the chats, and he can't even help it, sure I can hardly even go to the jacks and he's there asking me if I'm OK.' That got her back on side, a little, and she linked her arm in mine.

I sat in the middle, up the back, with no objections from either side. We eyed the recliners, to those with the extra paid privilege of lounging right back when watching the movie. We usually snuck over into them once the film had started, but there weren't three together, or even near each other, so we didn't bother with that today. Jasmine opened her backpack and fired over our cans and bags of popcorn, giving Joe's a sneaky shake before passing it over, 'Ya cheeky bitch' yelled as Fanta sprayed all over him, and the ground, and his seat.

I pushed my feet hard into the seat in front, and settled myself, all comfortable like, and began throwing popcorn into my mouth, head right back, lobbing them in, one after the other, when I tasted it, blood, and it was coming fast, all running into and catching at the back of my throat.

'Joe,' I said, his eyes straight ahead. I could feel it still running all over me, everywhere, I got to stand up, but I couldn't seem to keep my balance at all. Joe was at me, his arm around my waist. 'Joe,' I said again, and he was helping me out of the row.

'Jass, phone an ambulance,' Joe said, and I could just about see the hop of her, as she looked right at me, trying to take it in. 'Like fucking now, Jass.' She stumbled to get out of our way, rooted around in her pocket for her phone, followed close behind us.

'It'll be all right, bud,' Joe kept mumbling, over and over, 'we'll just get you out of here, you'll be all right.' But the brightness of the lobby, the coldness of it was too much, too quick, and I could hear a ringing, right in my ears, I could feel a sweat coming to my tongue, my face, and the blood was everywhere, all over my mouth and my T-shirt and I vomited, all over the gaff, right there in the lobby, my sick all blended into the blue speckled carpet. I knew, with Joe sat on the ground, hugging me in close to him, with the fuss, and the hype of cinema-staffed young ones surrounding us, that I hadn't said to feck to the cancer at all.

Joe

The warmth is there now, all muggy and too close, the sun trying hard to break through its blanket of grey. It's happening on up ahead, left at The College according to Dessie, place the *package* at the back of the bin at the edge of the pedestrianised square, then straight back, fairly lively like.

I have it tucked in at the band of my jeans, the gun, concealed in a bubble-padded envelope, folded over, to make it easier to hide. I can feel it every time I move, the shape of it digging right in. I tug at my hoodie again, stretching it down as far as I can, and check my watch, it's coming up on three. I quicken my pace, making sure that I won't be late.

But Carthy is there, snapping at my heels, under orders from Dessie, 'safety in numbers' he said, but I know it's to keep us in line, sussing us out to see where our loyalties lie, not fully trusting either of us, so it seems.

'How about it, bud, the boys are back in town,' Carthy laughs, trying to keep up with my strides. 'One for all and all for one. Yeah, Joe? Like it used to be? Remember? Remember, Joe?' And he's buzzing, hopping off his fucking head, the coke practically sweating out of him.

'Listen to fuck, Carthy, not another word. Nothing. Let's just get this done, yeah?' He looks at me, laughing, pretending to zip his lips, lock it and put it in his pocket, like when we were fucking kids.

'And while we're at it,' I say, turning right into him, 'what are you doing messing around with the Brophys?' He stops dead, a dullness tingeing the pink of his cheeks. 'Ma saw you, with his young one,' I continue, wanting to get this warning out of the way, so we could move on, and I could tell Ma I did my duty.

'Look, you're not going to . . .'

'Fuck no, I won't be saying anything, although I fucking should, after you ratted about the party.'

'What, no I never,' he says. I don't even care if he's telling the truth; I power on ahead, cursing Dessie for not letting me do this on my own, that he felt the need for a babysitter. And fucking Carthy to boot.

I feel his hand on my arm. I jerk it away, but it's persistent and strong and looks just like Sabine's. Fuck sake.

'Joe, you don't have to do this,' she says, no small chats today, just her getting straight to the point. Again. Carthy laughing, all relaxed again now, throwing me eyes, *get a load of your one* rolling right out of them. Sabine wedges herself between us, blocking him right out, but he doesn't get the hint.

'You really, really don't,' she says again, and she looks so scared, and she looks so hurt, and she looks like she's losing her faith in me.

'Just fuck off, yeah!' I say, stronger than I intended, harsher than I intended, and an 'Oooh, trouble in paradise,' exclamation from Carthy, enjoying his front-row seat.

'No,' she says, pulling at my arm, moving herself to block Carthy again. 'No, Joe, I won't fuck off.' She pulls me right round into her, makes me look at her, makes me look at her face. Sabine. 'Don't do this, Joe. Please. Just don't do it.' Her eyes are spilling with tears.

'I have to,' I say, putting my arms on her shoulders, trying to make her understand.

'If you do this, there is no going back, you fucking know that, don't you?' Her tears are still pouring, but her voice never wavers. I start to pull away from her. Pull away from her and her alternatives that I don't fucking want. 'Finn wouldn't have wanted any of this,' she shouts at my back. I give her a look, she has crossed over the line, but she is still coming and squaring right up to me. She hasn't a fucking clue.

'I am going now,' I say, looking her right in the eyes, her flinching at my cruelty. She is finally beginning to see. 'Don't follow. I don't want you there, I don't want you with me any more,' and I mean it. I really fucking do. She just stands there staring. Disbelief all over her face.

'Hate that,' Carthy says, patting her hard on the back, running to get back into my stride, to catch me right up, trying to put his arm round me, to show her that I'm part of him now. I shrug it straight off; Carthy could get to fuck too.

'Don't, Joe,' she half mumbles after me, a last half-hearted attempt, but I'm gone. Up past The College, a left turn straight after, just like Dessie told me I should.

Finn

Dr Kennedy called it a relapse. He said that the leukaemia came back, or was still floating around somewhere that couldn't be seen, or was never really gone at all in the first place, and I thought of all the talk about the chemo, it being a superdrug, it blasting the leukaemia all to shite, and I know now that it was all lies, because the chemo blasted absolutely feck all for me.

'It will be all right,' Joe said. I wasn't sure if he was talking to me or to himself, because none of this actually sounded all right at all.

A bone marrow transplant, Dr Kennedy called it. I was lucky, apparently, that Joe was a match for me, for my bone marrow. Lucky that we got to be let down again, when this all went to shite too.

I was back to the room on my own, and no one was allowed to touch me unless with special gloves, no one was allowed to speak to me unless with a special mask, and the front of the door was covered in plastic, and I wasn't allowed out, so I was trapped, just like Da. I'd been blasted with radiation for two weeks now. It was supposed to empty my bone marrow, to make way for Joe's, and I was afraid to trust that it would work, and then the operation Joe had, the big syringe in his back, to take all his marrow, to give to me, would all have been for nothing, a big waste of everyone's time, just like the chemo.

They rolled back in the coat stand, but this time with Joe's marrow swinging from the bag on the top. I was not even given the choice of the chair or the bed – I had to lie, with more machines, people in and out prodding me, checking me, and I hadn't the energy to tell them that I just wanted to be left alone.

Joe and Ma were with me all the time now, like ghosts at the end of the bed, in their gloves and masks. I wished that they'd let me be, even for a bit, I wished I could tell them to go away, that I didn't want them to be there, to see me cry, and scream in pain, and vomit, all the time now, making my throat all wretched and raw. I didn't want them to see any of that, at all. But they did, and they stayed every day. Just their eyes staring at me over the top of their masks.

I was just so tired all the time now, but I couldn't even sleep, with Joe and Ma's faithful watch, I couldn't seem to ever relax, at all, in case they'd think there was something else wrong with me, as if, if I slept, it would worry Ma that I'd never wake up, and I couldn't do that to her, she was already completely broken as it was.

Joe

It's safer during the day, Dessie had said, with everyone else going on about their business, not bothered to fuck by two teenagers crossing paths at the side of The College. I keep my hand at the band of my jeans, take position beside the bin, watch the second hand count down to three o'clock, crouch while Carthy stands, and pull at the broken hatch, swing the casing open, placing the package right in at the back, well out of sight.

'Did ya take a look in it?' he's asking, skipping along beside me as we make our retreat, across the square. 'I bet ya did, didn't ya?' he's saying, tapping at the side of his nose. I push my hands deep into my pockets and power ahead, but he's keeping up, nudging me, spitting right into my ear. I'm pushing him off but he keeps at it, with a 'Look, Joe, fucking look,' and I am, looking, at the hard, determined bulk right there approaching us, fucking Da. What's he even doing here, another fucking watchdog, can he not just let me do this one thing on my own, and if he thinks he's taking over here, that I'm just going to leave him and Carthy to it, he can fuck right off.

It's the creep of it that hits; the bang, from somewhere behind, loud, close, the ring of it right in my ears, the echo of it right though my entire being. I turn back to look, to the source of it, a gloved hand still outstretched, the gun then dropped, skidded to my feet, and a 'Fuck, Joe?' from Carthy, whispered, a plea, asking me what it is he should do, and the singed stench of burning, and my heart is electric, and the heat of the blood is all over my face, my hands, my chest, and a sharp heavy weight is all over my body, making it harder and harder to breathe.

Finn

Dr Kennedy, Ma and Joe all hovered around the side of me. I knew, I could feel it hopping off Ma, well before Dr Kennedy even opened his mouth, that there was something really, really wrong with me.

'I'm sorry, Finn, the transplant didn't take,' he said, all matter of fact, just like that. As if he was reading out his shopping list or a Lego instruction manual, and putting it out there, 'didn't take', as if I even had a clue what he was on about at all. But I knew, by the sudden grip of Ma and Joe's hands, that it wasn't something good.

'It is always a risky procedure, and with these type of things, when the cancer cells are hidden like yours were, Finn, it was impossible to tell that they were there at all,' he said.

'Do I have to have more treatment,' I asked, not sure I could take any more of that, not sure that I wanted any of that at all.

'No, son, there will be no more treatment,' he said. 'Your mum and Joe here will go through with you what we discussed.' I looked over to Ma, and to Joe, and Ma had dropped to the ground. Nurse Sarah rushed over, put her arms around Ma's waist, and stayed with her like that. Joe didn't do anything, he just kept rubbing his back, where the needle took his marrow, being so still, except for that, rubbing it over and over, and the look like he wanted to bust somebody, but neither could speak to me.

'Am I going home so?' I asked, not thinking I'd be able to make it home; my legs, and arms, the whole skeleton of me ached, burned, any time I moved. I didn't think I'd be able to walk to the bus either, or stay on it without getting sick.

'No, son, you'll be staying here with us,' and I knew by the way he said it, by the grief of Ma and Joe, filling the entirety of the room with their rawness, that I was never going to be going home again.

'What about Da,' I said, the panic now of not being able to see him. 'Will he be able to come to see me?' Joe was at my side then.

'I'm on it, Finney, I'll do my best,' and that confirmed it for me right there. I held on to his hand on my shoulder, and Ma came over and got into the bed beside me, and I hated what I had done to her, and Joe, and Da. Hated that I caused them all of this. And Ma, how was I supposed to act around her? How could I stop all this reaching her? How was she going to be able to cope, with me gone? And I was going to be gone, wasn't I? I wanted to ask Dr Kennedy where. *Gone where?* I wanted to shout at him, scream at him. He had stepped away from the bed, to let us have our space, but not before I caught a glimpse of the chart in his arms. My chart, it was flipped open on a page that read *End of Life Care.*

The end of my life.
The end of me.
The end of Finn O'Reilly.

Joe

'Joe.' Sabine. She's down by my side, and people are gathering, babies crying, doors opening, windows, phones out, an 'all right, mister' shouted from somewhere distant.

'Fuck.' She's screaming and shaking now. I try to get up, but I'm weighed down by Carthy, his blood spurted all over me.

And Da is there, dropped right down beside us, pulling at Carthy, rolling him right off, placing his head in his lap, with a growl piercing at the back of his throat, 'The gun, Joe,' he says, his hand outstretched, 'quick.' I reach to pick it up, the tremble of it in my fingers, and he grabs it, wipes it on his T-shirt and clasps it in his own.

'He had you,' he says, barely a rasp, and all I see is the gun that he's wiped clean of me, 'this is what he does,' he continues, the vulnerability of him expanding as he clings to Carthy, pulling him closer, 'it's never just a drop,' holding my gaze. I want to say something, do something, but I'm shivering and fragmented and I can't catch my breath.

'You need to go,' he says, giving me my cue. 'Get him the fuck out of here,' he yells, clutching at Carthy, cradling him now, and Sabine is behind me, her two arms clasped, linked around my torso, pulling, her knee dug right into my back, pulling at the resisted weight of me.

'Get the fuck up,' she shouts, getting more urgent, still trying to pull me up as flashes of blue and ever-closing sirens encroach in on our space, a larger crowd now gathered, with Mas' fingers shielding the eyes of their young ones as they try to peek through. She takes off her jumper now and begins wiping my hands and my face, zipping up my jacket over the crimson splash of evidence now graffiting my top. Da stays right where he is. There with Carthy cradled into him, sitting in his pool of blood, staring straight ahead, waiting for that flash to catch up to him. Sabine's guiding me now. Has me folded right into her, she's gripping my hand tight, her fingers wound right around, not letting go of mine.

'Dessie never would have let you go,' Da whispers as I take one last look, Sabine still moving me away.

'Keep walking,' she orders with her arm around my waist, keeping our heads down as she forces me in the side door of the Hangman's Inn, right down to the back and into the jacks, and sits me on a cracking toilet seat. It's his blood all over me. Carthy's. All over me, warm and hot and his. Covering me, I can't get the smell and the feel and the heat of it off of me.

And she's there, Sabine, pulling reams of tissue, dampening them under the tap, locking herself in with me. She unzips my jacket then, and takes off my top, and runs the tissues over my face and my neck and my chest; she dumps them all, the tissues, my top and her jumper, into the overflowing sanitary bin. But he's still there, Carthy, still there between us. Part of me, part of us. We were supposed to stick together. We were supposed to look out for each other, we were supposed to be one for all and all for one, once upon a time. And I'm remembering the first time Da was inside, Carthy knocked in with a snack box from the Nippy Chippy, the first time his Ma was missing in action, it was a naggin of vodka and a packet of smokes.

Sabine is still wiping, wiping the last of his blood right off me, I'm watching it flush, disappearing, just like that, and my breath is catching, and Sabine is getting closer, shushing me, over and over, *ssh ssh ssh*, the rhythm of it, right into my ear. I try to level my breath, to match in time with hers. Try to stop it racing, running too far ahead of me. But Carthy's blood is still fresh on my chest, and I feel the ache of it, the physical pull of it, breaking me completely apart, and I ball my fist in tight to my forehead, digging the knuckles right in, feeling the bone on bone, rubbing it harder, pushing it harder, in between gulps of air that I just can't seem to catch, and she puts her hand up to mine, presses it right there, and my fist is loosening, my hand is opening, being pulled to hers, I match mine to hers, her look never wavers, we are all matching, me and her, her and me.

Then she wraps her arms, all the way around, and I can feel all her tears soaking into my chest, I want to keep them right there, as I cry into her hair. She never even said, *I fucking told you so*. Sabine.

Finn

Joe said that the warden wouldn't let Da come to visit. He had asked, pleaded, but he wouldn't budge. That Guard was still in a coma see, and it didn't look like he was going to make it, just like me.

I wanted to visit him instead. I had been, twice already with Ma, but Dr Kennedy really didn't think that was such a good idea. The nosebleeds were getting worse, heavier, and my breathing still wasn't right, and I got tired, all the feckin' time, even from just walking to the bathroom. Nurse Sarah said I could use a bedpan, some horrible grey cardboard hat yoke, and I didn't even think it would hold all your stuff, that it would just dissolve right on through, leaving even more of a mess. No way was I using it anyway. There was a wheelchair beside the bed, to make that journey easier, from my bed to the bathroom, but I'd ask Joe for his arm instead, just to lean on, to the bathroom door, every time, even if it made my breath all jumpy, or my head all sweaty, I was not using no cardboard bowl or a wheelchair. I didn't think I really wanted Da to see me like this anyway. He couldn't handle seeing me with no hair, let alone looking at the sight of me now. I didn't know what that would do to him.

I was allowed to write a letter, one that could explain it all. Ma said she'd give it to him on the next visit, but what do you say to your Da, when you know you are never going to see him again?

'Just tell him you love him, Finney, that's all you need,' Ma said, barely keeping it together, and I wrapped my arms around her tight, taking in the whole of her, my Ma.

Later, when it was just me, I opened up the big black hardbound sketchpad that Nurse Sarah got me. 'A place to write all your favourite things,' she said, 'it helps,' she said, 'promise.' I took up my black pen and began, and it flowed, all right out of me, full of ice creams, and sandcastles, and Joe, and Ma, and I let it just keep on flowing.

'What ya doing, bud.' Joe came in to the side of me, coffee cup in his hand; I edged it close to him, and he laughed, really, really laughed, and gave me a big hug.

'That's fucking amazing so that is,' he said. 'A fucking legend, that's what you are, Finn,' he said, slapping me on the back like Da would do.

'Will you illustrate it?' I asked.

'Of course I will,' he said, taking my hand. 'I'd fucking love to,' he said, squeezing my hand in his.

'I was thinking, maybe like a comic, see I've boxed it all out here, at the back, but we could lay it out properly, all neat like, here at the front.' I looked to him, to see what he thought. I needed him to think that it was OK, I needed to be able to do this. Have something to show, have something for Ma, and Da when I was gone, a bit of me, and Joe, right here in this book.

'I think it's the best idea I've ever heard,' Joe said, and I knew that he meant it. Joe always meant everything that he said. Always.

'Right, we'll do one per page, I think, that way I can get us all in, get all the detail like.' He started to sketch out his ideas. 'I'll do a rough draft first, see if you like it, then you can change it if you want, it can be our little project.'

He started to busy himself, his hand etching out the outlines, of all my favourite things. I leaned my head back. I felt calm for the first time since I knew, for the first time since I learned that this was all going to stop for me. I closed my eyes and listened to the scratch of Joe's pen, just as if we were at home, me listening from my top bunk as he sketched into the night.

Joe

I watched as you took your last breath, held your hand as it turned cold, watched as death crawled into you, suffocating you, to never let you go.

The funeral was like Granda's. A fucking old man's funeral. With a teddy on the coffin that you hadn't seen in years and a jersey of a team you'd long since abandoned. There was none of you there.

Dr Flynn had to give Ma an injection. It blocked her feelings from reaching the surface for those few hours. She stared blankly at the priest and clenched on to me so tightly her fingerprints bruised my arm. I don't know what she remembers, I haven't asked.

They let Da come, but he wasn't allowed to sit with us. He had to sit down the back, chained and wedged between two Guards with batons and *stay the fuck away* muscles. They wouldn't let him talk to us after, either. They just shuffled him back into their van as he screamed and wailed and cursed. They wouldn't even let him touch the coffin. How was he supposed to say goodbye?

I wish I'd asked you what you wanted.

I wish we'd played songs you could dance to.

I wish we'd brought balloons, and colour and fun.

If we'd had you cremated, I'd still have part of you here.

I could have done something cool with your ashes. Like skydived, or brought you on Space Mountain, or sprinkled them over Principal Kelly's car in the school car park. You would have laughed your head off at that.

Why the fuck did I let you have an old man's funeral?

Finn

Joe had a playlist made, of all our favourites, and played them through his phone, put on shuffle, so we didn't know which one was coming up next, wrapped up like a surprise. Dr Kennedy must have known what Joe was doing, because he brought in his Bluetooth speaker, and didn't care when we turned it up loud and filled the whole place with our booming beats.

I wished that I could get up and dance with Ma, but I was so, so tired and weak. I got Joe to prop me right up with some pillows, extras and all brought in from the nurses' station, and the back of the bed up as high as it would go, so at least it looked like I was sat up.

The smell of chips was still in the air; I had mine with extra vinegar, and a battered sausage dipped in curry sauce, and Joe ran across the road after, to get us all big ice-cream cones, with extra sauce and sprinkles. Not the same as Mr Whippy, but not too bad either. I joked with Joe after, that it was just like Ma's favourite film, *The Green Mile*, me eating my last meal and all that, but I don't think he got it, well, he didn't laugh anyway, and he just clenched his fists and stared straight ahead, not saying even anything at all.

The priest was called in. To read my Last Rites, last right to what, I wanted to know. But the priest was so nice and kind and gentle and it made Ma feel better, I could see some of her pain being lifted away with the words that the priest said to her and to me. But it didn't do anything for Joe, that I knew, because he kept his back to us, and his face was harder than ever, and he looked just so much like Da.

Da was allowed to ring after, and Ma and Joe left, and the nurses made sure it was just me and him, put a 'Do Not Disturb' sign right on the door, to make sure that we were not interrupted. We talked about memories of us, and us all, of funfairs and parties and Christmas and the flats, not once talking about what was going to happen to me.

'I wish I could be there, son,' he said. I could hear his voice crack and he coughed to shake it all away.

'But you are here, Da,' I said, and I hugged my Transformer closer to me, and the cracks were getting louder and his voice was getting harder to hear, but then I heard them call 'Time's up,' on the other end of the phone, and the last words from my Da ever to me.

'You were always the very best of us all.'

Joe

I had it wrapped. Ready for your birthday, for when you came home. Now, a year on, I take it out from its hiding place, from behind the pots and pans in the corner press, dismantling the woven seal of protective cobwebs as I do. One of its foiled corners jabs at the inside of my thumb, reminding me to beware, reminding me that this still holds the power to hurt. I make my way to our bedroom, your parcel held tight to my chest, trying to feel the essence of you, straight through the layers of dust-shiny packaging. Up onto the top bunk, still exactly as you left it, Ma too terrified to box you up yet, to close another lid and leave you in darkness.

I take the T-shirt you slept in from underneath your pillow, all ordinary, grey, balled at the armpits from too much washing; not one thing about it represents anything about you at all. I hold it up tight to my face and inhale, trying to fill myself with the scent of you, but it's long gone – all I smell is the Lynx spray of me, and Ma's burnt toast from this morning's breakfast, and the memory of your scent is tainted anyway, forever replaced with clean, and bleach, and antiseptic, that sticks right at the back of my throat.

I've been sleeping up here more recently. Trying to keep myself connected to you, what you woke up to every morning. I try to feel you through touching absolutely everything you'd pinned to the wall and the celling. And it works. Sometimes.

I can hear Sabine chatting to Ma before I see her. In hushed tones, trying not to reach me.

'Joe,' she says opening the door, in a question. She looks all uncomfortable, half in, half out of the room, shielding her body with the door jamb, not wanting to encroach on me, or my space, if I didn't want it.

'It's all right,' I call, and I move myself over, to make room for her. She's up in an instant, connecting herself to me, arm to arm, hip to hip, her hand reaching for mine.

'He should be here,' I say, turning my head to look at her, and she coils her fingers tighter around mine. 'He should be brushing us off to go out with his mates, smoke his first fag, get his first shift, or whatever the fuck he wanted.' I release it all, in one long breath, and Sabine just pulses my hand tighter, letting me get it all out.

Ma had a cake and all. That chocolate caterpillar log that you used to love from Tesco. Put in thirteen candles, I watched as she blew them out, closed her eyes to make a wish, a wish that I knew would never materialise. I try to imagine what you'd be like. Would you even want a caterpillar cake any more? Would you act too cool for school in front of your friends? Would you stay out too late, me sent after to drag you back home? The trying to picture all this is too much. I'm finding it too hard to remember you as you were; it's enough as it is, I don't need the added weight of this too.

'He should be fucking here,' I say again, and I take my hand from hers and wrap it back around his present. Squeezing it tighter, crushing my ribs, feeling the weight of him, of it all, pressed tight on me. I can feel Sabine releasing me, unwinding my arms, and my hands, and placing her head on my chest, beside your present, breathing with me in and out, whispering into me, into my heart, words of calm, words of still, and I can smell the fresh vanilla of her hair, and I release.

'Open it,' she says, positioning herself beside me again, nudging her elbow gently into my side, but I'm not sure that I want to.

'Open it,' she says again, more forcefully this time. I pull myself up, she leans into me, and I begin to tear at the paper, until the black hardbound sketchbook is there looking right at me. Daring me to open it up. My hand hovers for a while, feeling that magnetic pull of you, trying to ignore it. But your force as always is too strong, and I open that very first page.

/

Ma is there, trying to carry on as normal, to act as if today is the same as any other day. Sure who would remember significant dates, significant memories, who still holds compassion and kind words and thoughtfulness a year later. She wipes down the counter, with a methodical, rhythmic action of her hands. She catches me and smiles a little, at least knowing that I'll acknowledge or understand her pain.

'Ma,' I say, placing the sketchbook on the counter, drying it first with the back of my sleeve. She wipes her own hands on the calves of her trousers and pulls it closer to her.

'What's this,' she asks, taking quick glances my way, but afraid to take her eyes off the book, his book, at the same time.

'Open it,' I say, me and Sabine shooting excited glances, waiting for her to catch sight of you again, but she is hesitating, not liking the unknown of it, not liking the surprise of it. Not liking surprises any more, at all.

'Go on,' I say again, nudging it even closer to her. She pulls back the front cover and immediately lets a cry out, pulling her two hands up to her face, then touching you gently, not quite believing it. You are looking straight at us. I used colour for this one; black ink would never ever do you justice, the colour of you always too bright, too hard to capture.

'Joe,' she says, but keeping her eyes on you, running her finger over every shaded line of your face, your hair, your eyes. 'Joe, he's here,' she cries, drinking in every ounce of you. We sit opposite her in silence, watching her turn page after page, getting to discover you all over again.

'We're doing it, Ma,' I point down to the book, 'all of it, it's his bucket list,' I say, my voice cracking, 'me and Sabine,' I take her hand in mine, 'and we want you to do it too.' She runs straight around the counter and hugs us both to her so tight. The book bent back on the last page, on her, in all her grief. Hair straggled by her face, fag held loosely by her side, and the deep-edged sadness of her face and the gouged-out hurt of her eyes, as if someone else is carelessly wearing her skin. I'd forgotten I'd even drawn it, captured just a week before you died. Raw and powerful and true, with the angry bold lines of my charcoal. A thought bubble hovers over her, showing how it used to be. Of Ma holding you close, tussling your hair, laughing, joking, haunting us. Your words are there underneath:

Ma. Don't ever forget.

I love you.

/

'Pat, I'm off,' Ma shouts over the counter, into the back room.

'What? Annie, what the fuck,' Pat says, running out, leaving the blare of *Match of the Day* filtering through.

'You'll just have to take over,' she says, throwing the stale, stinking dishcloth beside him on the counter.

'But I'm watching the match,' he complains, nodding his head towards the haven of the back room.

'Sure put it on out here,' she says, walking herself out of the door.

'Annie,' he shouts after her, 'Annie come on,' he shouts again, but she's out and linking her arms with us, me and Sabine. Ned is out by the door, hopped out of his seat to reach his lighter that fell on the ground, quickly hopping back in when he sees us coming. Ma holds the door for him.

'All right there, Ned,' I say, tapping him on the back of the chair.

'Leaving so soon, Annie, Pat won't be liking that,' he says, laughing at the state of it all, thinking it is absolutely hilarious, truth be told.

'Well, Pat can fucking lump it,' Ma says, giving Ned a wink. He grabs her arm on his way in the door.

'How you holding up today, love, birthdays are a tough one.' We all do a double take, and Ma wraps her hands around his neck fiercely, planting a kiss right on his cheek. I actually see him blush, embarrassed now, pushing her away.

'Ah would ya get off that now, Annie, a good memory for dates is all,' but he can't hide the curl of the smile at his lips, the glow it has given to Ma.

'Right so, Joe, where to first,' she asks. But I'm already leading them down to Mr Whippy, following his music-box sounds, getting ready for page number one.

Finn

I thought that it was nearly time to go, and I ran my fingers through the bucket of sand, straight all the way from Dollymount Strand. Picking it up, and sprinkling it right through my fingers. Tickling the inside of my palm.

'I wish it could have been the real thing,' Joe said, choking the words out, but I didn't really care about that at all. I could smell it. Feel it. Remember it, and all right here from this bucket Joe brought.

And I thought that it was nearly time to go, and I tried not to think about how Da couldn't come or how I didn't get all the things done that I wanted to do, or how I would never again see Ma or Joe, and I just hoped that they would all be OK.

And I thought that it was nearly time to go. I could feel my breath leaving, getting lighter and lighter, and Ma and Joe's warmth, either side of me, and I hugged my Transformer close up to my chest, and I grabbed one last fistful of Dollymount sand, and the taste of sweet ice cream was still fresh on my lips, and yes, now I was ready to go.

Breath in.

And out.

Breath in.

And out.

And out.
And out.
All out, surrounded by love.

Joe

People are still afraid to say that you died. That you are dead. They say you passed away, as if you are just gone somewhere unreachable, that you are still here.

Sorry for your loss, I hear over and over. What does that even mean? Your loss? It gets stuck right in the knot of anger balled tight in my chest, because lost is tied to hope, which is connected to found, as if you will be returned to me at some point, so how can I ever let you go, if you are still there, holding on, waiting for me to find you.

They say that time heals, but that's just so fucking wrong. There's this big gaping hole that will never be filled, that will never be healed, but it does become more bearable, I will give them that.

I'm stood here now, with Ma and Sabine, all stood at the mural that I painted of him, right after he died, all big and bold, at the side of our tower. He's looking at us, all strong blacks and greys, with 'Just Joe' signed down at the bottom-right corner. There are flowers here too, and candles, signatures and messages from all over the flats, and his school, and I couldn't think of a better reminder of him.

'You ready, love,' Ma asks, turning to the very last thing on our list, and the lightness we all feel now. The loss of you more bearable, the passing of you more comfortable, as we still have you right here; every time we enact this, you come bursting through, refusing to be forgotten or ignored. The vividness of you breathing life and energy into the rest of us that you left behind.

'Ready, Ma,' I say, putting my arm around her shoulders, her leaning on me, me leaning on her, both of us protecting, shielding the other.

We've spun in a trolley round the back of the flats, eaten screwballs with sprinkles and sauce, snuck into The Plex, with plastic bags of popcorn, fizzy worms and Coke, fresh from kicking sandcastles at Dollymount Strand, and we walk my bike up to the top of the hill, and with Ma on the back and Sabine on the bars, I cycle like the clappers down Captains Hill.

Acknowledgements

Firstly, to the phenomenal Louisa Joyner, whose name should be on the front cover next to mine. Thank you for being so intuitive, encouraging and patient, and for challenging me to deliver the very best book that I possibly could.

To my amazing agent, Sophie Lambert, 'what's for you won't go by you' never being more true in this case. Thank you for *getting* the book, and me, and for taking the boys into your heart immediately.

To Louise Buckley, for believing in this book from the very beginning and advocating for it with such passion and care.

To the whole team at Faber, who have made the process of publishing my debut so enjoyable. Libby, Seán, Niriksha, Phoebe, Sophie, Lauren and a whole host of people I know I'm forgetting. Thank you for being so fantastic and kind and for never making me feel like I hadn't a clue what I was doing.

To Claire, who copy-edited with such sensitivity; to Djinn, for her eagle-eyed proofread; and to Anna Morrison, for the absolute stunner of a cover. Becky, thank you, you have captured the heart of *Boys Don't Cry* so perfectly.

To Kildare County Council Arts Services, for their continued support, the National Arts Council of Ireland, whose literature bursary award was invaluable in allowing me the time and space to complete this book, and to the beyond-wonderful Ferdia Mac Anna, who I was privileged to be paired with through the Words Ireland national mentoring programme. Thank you all for your belief in me and this book.

To the incredible University of Glasgow Creative Writing Department, Colin, Zoë, Carolyn and Laura, thank you for pushing me out of my comfort zone and for giving me the confidence to trust in my own writing voice. This book would not be in existence without you.

To my wonderful colleagues at St Anne's Primary School, thank you for always being so supportive.

To my writing tribes, the inspirational Dooligans, with our leader, Sarah Moore Fitzgerald, and my beloved VWG. I honestly am so grateful for all your encouragement, love, friendship and, most importantly, making me laugh every single day. You all know who you are.

To my early readers Wiz and Julia, for giving me the confidence to keep going. To Cat, who after reading my first round of edits convinced me it wasn't all a total pile of shite, and to Dan, who kept me sane in the roller coaster that is being on submission. I hope you all know how much I appreciate and value your generous friendships.

To my beautiful family and biggest cheerleaders – Mam, Dad, Sarah, Oisín and Rónán – who show me what it means to be unconditionally loved, every single day.

To my gorgeous Da, who unfortunately never got to see

this book in print, but whose inspiration is all over these pages, who believed without question that one person can make a difference, and that we should all at least try.

To every single nurse working in end-of-life care. Please know that your compassion, respect and kindness means so very much, and will never be forgotten.

To Dermot, my absolute rock and very best friend, for knowing that I would see this day, even when I didn't believe it myself, especially when I didn't believe it myself.

To my Molly and Charlie, showing me the fierce friendship, loyalty and inseparability of a true sibling bond like no other.

And finally, to all the readers who find this in their hands, thank you for taking the chance.